A woman with ha[...] crossed the street towar[...] side. Everything around him slowed—the breeze, the beating of his heart, time itself. Like a sniper never straying from the target, he locked his gaze on her. Her long locks whipped across her face, but he didn't need to see the narrow nose and pouty lips to figure out who she was. He'd have recognized her laugh anywhere.

Jilly.

Jillian stopped in the middle of the street and her spine stiffened.

The boy at her side tugged her hand and pulled her toward the sidewalk.

She shifted her weight and angled her head in his direction.

His breath stalled in his chest. The breeze beat back her silken strands and exposed her ivory skin. A mossy green gaze found his, and the full mouth he had loved to kiss fell open for a brief moment before she snapped it closed.

He took a few steps toward her but stopped when she pressed her mouth into a firm line. She was so close the breeze carried her scent toward him—vanilla and lavender and just Jillian. He found spare change in his pocket and he jingled it, waiting for a sign on what to do next.

Praise for Danielle M. Haas

"I never connected with a PTSD victim until I read *SECOND TIME AROUND*. Ms. Haas' descriptions of Jonah's feelings made my skin prickle and my stomach clench as I felt his anxiety. If anyone ever deserved a Happy Ever After, it is Jonah and Jilly."

~Becky L.

~*~

"The author pulls you in from the first paragraph. Will Jonah be able to adjust to civilian life? Will Jillian find happiness? Each chapter brings you closer to finding how past hurts will affect their future."

~Celeste C.

~*~

"Danielle M Haas is the master of sweet romance novels. *SECOND TIME AROUND* is beautifully written and gave me all the feels."

~Olivia A.

~*~

"Danielle M Haas captures your heart in *SECOND TIME AROUND*. This spellbinding story of a swoon-worthy, war-torn hero and a heartbroken, single mother carrying a devastating secret pulls at your heartstrings. *SECOND TIME AROUND* had me rooting for Jonah and Jillian's love story to the end!"

~Samantha K.

~*~

"An enemies-to-lovers, small town romance, *SECOND TIME AROUND* is a sweet, sexy romp, filled with enough twists and turns to keep you guessing until the happily ever after waiting at the end."

~Laura C.

Second Time Around

by

Danielle M. Haas

The Sheffields, Book 1

Second Time Around

Cover Art by *Tina Lynn Stout*

The Wild Rose Press, Inc.
PO Box 708
Adams Basin, NY 14410-0708
Visit us at www.thewildrosepress.com

Publishing History
First Sweetheart Rose Edition, 2019
Print ISBN 978-1-5092-2893-5
Digital ISBN 978-1-5092-2894-2

The Sheffields, Book 1
Published in the United States of America

Dedication

To Scott, my loving husband,
whose unwavering support has given me
the confidence to put pen to paper.

To my beautiful children,
Abigail and Vaughn,
thank you for inspiring me to fulfill my dreams
so I could always encourage you to follow yours.

To all of my friends and family
who've cheered me on the last few years.
Especially my mom
for being my biggest cheerleader
and constant springboard,
Celeste for being my bulldog
always fighting for me to keep going,
and my Swan Sister, Sam.
Without you,
my words would still just make sentences on a screen
instead of weaving together
the first story my heart ever led me to write.

Chapter One

Anywhere but here. Why can't I be anywhere but here?

The heat of the midday sun beating down was like a brushstroke of warmth compared to the heat radiating from the curious eyes scorching his skin. Jonah lowered his head and locked his gaze on the thorny weeds snaking through the cracked cement of the sidewalk. People from Smithview, Ohio, would be happy he'd finally come home, but they'd also want to know every damn detail of what happened in Iraq.

Details he had never told another soul.

Details that haunted his dreams and occupied his wounded mind like he'd occupied the dry desert for the past twelve years.

Hurried footsteps fell past him, and he buried his hands in his pockets. His baseball hat hid his face from people passing by, and he took quick, shallow breaths to fight off the annoyance crawling over his flesh. A soft tinkle of laughter floated on the gentle August breeze and skimmed over his sweat-slicked skin. Jonah lifted his head, and he flitted his gaze past the old stone courthouse in the middle of the town square and landed on the book store Jillian owned. The door was closed, and no one lingered near the storefront. Disappointment crushed him with the weight of an avalanche.

Hunching his shoulders toward his ears, he turned

in the opposite direction. A woman with hair the color of golden wheat crossed the street toward him with a young boy at her side. Everything around him slowed—the breeze, the beating of his heart, time itself. Like a sniper never straying from the target, he locked his gaze on her. Her long locks whipped across her face, but he didn't need to see the narrow nose and pouty lips to figure out who she was. He'd have recognized her laugh anywhere.

Jilly.

Jillian stopped in the middle of the street and her spine stiffened.

The boy at her side tugged her hand and pulled her toward the sidewalk.

She shifted her weight and angled her head in his direction.

His breath stalled in his chest. The breeze beat back her silken strands and exposed her ivory skin. A mossy green gaze found his, and the full mouth he had loved to kiss fell open for a brief moment before she snapped it closed.

He took a few steps toward her but stopped when she pressed her mouth into a firm line. She was so close the breeze carried her scent toward him—vanilla and lavender and just Jillian. He found spare change in his pocket and he jingled it, waiting for a sign on what to do next. If her pinched lips and creased brow were any indication, she'd rather tell him to get the hell away from her than stop in the middle of town for a friendly chat.

Damn it, go say hi. I look like an idiot standing here staring.

The little boy craned his neck toward Jonah, and

his mop of dark waves swayed with the motion. Almond-colored eyes turned inquisitive, and he tugged Jillian's hand harder in his direction. In three steps, they came to a stop in front of Jonah on the cracked sidewalk.

"Hi, Jillian." People milled around them, but for once, they didn't bother him. His words were thick in his throat and came out with a soft growl.

"It's been a long time, Jonah."

The chilliness in her voice beat back the heat from the afternoon sun, and his skin puckered with goose bumps.

She dropped the boy's hand and collected her hair in her palms before sweeping it over her shoulder, working her fingers between the tangles.

The pressure in his chest eased a fraction. Jillian always played with her hair when she was nervous. The small gesture was enough to settle his nerves from a jangled ball of strobing lights about to explode to a single strand occasionally blinking its distress.

He tore his gaze from the face that haunted his dreams since the day he'd left town and focused on the boy by her side. "Hi there. I'm Jonah." He extended a hand, and the boy's firm grip surprised him.

"I'm Sam."

"Nice to meet you." Jonah noted the wide smile and the smattering of freckles across the bridge of his nose. "You must be Jillian's son. I've been told a lot about you."

"You have?" Sam's eyes widened.

Jillian placed an arm around Sam's shoulders and pulled him close. "How did you know he's my son?"

Jonah curved up his lips on one side. "You know

3

how much the women in my family love to talk. They've mentioned your Sam a few times, and he looks so much like you. I assumed you were him."

Sam angled his chin and glanced at Jillian. "Is he serious? We don't look anything alike."

Jillian ruffled Sam's hair and laughed. "Trust me. I'm aware of how much you look like your dad. It's annoyed me for eight long years."

Sam's grin eased Jonah's reservations about seeing Jillian his first day back in town, and he smiled with the mother-son duo. He lifted a shoulder in a shrug. "I see a lot of your mom in your features. The freckles, the mouth, and the way you tilt your head to the side when you're listening. You got all those from her."

"How do you know my mom?" Sam scrunched his nose from the glare of the sun.

"Jonah and I are old friends," Jillian cut in.

A knot formed in the bottom of his gut at her casual reference to their past.

"Are you as old as my mom?"

The words poured from a smile as wide as the Grand Canyon. Damn, he liked this kid.

"Samuel!" Jillian fisted her hands on her hips but a grin lit her face.

Jonah chuckled. "How old do you think I am?"

"That's a dangerous question." Jillian quirked her brow. "You might think thirty is young, but to an eight-year-old, anything over twenty is downright ancient."

Jonah winced and grabbed his chest, stumbling backward a few steps. "Ouch, you wound me." Mischief sparked in Sam's dark honey-colored eyes, and Jonah fought the urge to ruffle his tousled hair the same way Jillian had done moments before. The

4

mischief quickly morphed into recognition.

"Wait, you're Jonah? Meg's brother? The Marine who's having the big party tonight at the inn?" Sam's words came out in a rush, and he bounced up and down on his toes.

Panic zigzagged across Jonah's bones, and all the moisture in his mouth evaporated. The reality of what his mom must be planning crashed down, and he closed his eyes. She'd told him she'd planned a small dinner with him and his sisters. He should have known better. Annie Sheffield never did anything small. He swallowed his initial reaction. "You're a lot more excited about a party than I am. Are you going?"

Sam kicked a stone lying on the sidewalk with the toe of his sneaker. "No. My dad's picking me up for the weekend. I wish I could go, though. Everyone in town is going."

Jonah shifted his gaze back to Jillian. If his mom's insane idea of a coming home party would bring Jillian to his door, the hell he'd experience with all those people around would be worth it. "Will you be there?" Redness swirled across her cream-colored cheeks and sparked a flame of longing in the pit of his stomach. A knee-bending, soul-consuming longing only Jillian could ignite.

Jillian's pink tongue swiped across her bottom lip.

He bit back a groan.

"I don't think so." Clearing her throat, she broke eye contact and focused on her son. "Sam, why don't you head to the market and get your snacks? I'll be inside in a minute."

Sam waved goodbye to Jonah.

Jillian's gaze followed him until he entered the

store.

Silent tension pulsed between them. He dropped his gaze to his shuffling feet, and sweat broke out on the back of his neck. He peeked from under the bill of his hat and rubbed his palm over the two-day growth on his cheek. "You look good, Jilly."

"Don't call me that."

Her icy whisper stood in stark contrast to the late summer heat and sent chills up his arm. "Please, can we talk?" He reached out a hand.

Recoiling, she wrapped her arms around herself.

He dropped his arm to his side, unsure of himself once again.

"What is there to talk about?" She glanced up. "I haven't seen you in twelve years, Jonah. You can't come back to town and act like nothing happened between us. Just because time has passed doesn't mean the wounds healed."

The lightning that pierced his heart seconds ago exploded, and a flash of a memory branded his brain—a memory of darkness and death and despair. "What do you know about wounds? About needing to get over the past before you can even begin to think about a future? What happened in high school is a drop in a bucket compared to the hell I've seen."

Tears hovered at the brim of Jillian's lashes, and she took a step backward. Her sandal-clad foot teetered on the edge of the curb, and she swung her arms forward to keep her balance.

The angry blast of a horn sounded from the street. Jonah grabbed her hand and pulled her close. A whoosh of breath left her mouth and caressed his neck. He lowered his hand to the small of her back, wrapping himself in her soft curves and the familiar touch of his first love.

A flattened hand pressed against his chest and pushed.

Even as she pushed him away, her touch caused his breath to hitch.

"You can let me go. I need to find Sam."

"Please, can we talk?" He'd made her cry. Or at least had almost made her cry before she'd almost fallen into oncoming traffic to get away.

The muscles in her slender body stiffened, and she stared past the shadows of his hat and directly into his eyes. "If you think the hell I went through is merely a drop in the bucket, then we have nothing to talk about. Welcome home, Jonah."

The harsh tone of her voice made a mockery of her words and crushed his hope of rekindling what they'd once had. The subtle sway of her hips in her cotton dress caught his attention as she walked away.

Again.

A tug on his T-shirt yanked his shoulder back. His senses prickled, and the strobing nerves from before returned with a vengeance, lighting up his neurons. He grabbed on to the rough skin attached to his shirt, spun, and yanked the arm in a circle over his head. He balanced his weight on the balls of his feet, ready to strike the person who belonged to the hand he held. He glanced down and into the wide, terrified eyes of his baby sister.

"Jeez, Jonah. What the hell's your problem?"

He dropped Meg's hand and rubbed the back of his neck. The hot, muggy air coated the inside of his mouth and refused to slide down his throat. Shallow breaths coursed in and out of his body. But he couldn't get enough air into his lungs to calm his racing heart. He squeezed his eyes shut, but the images from before crashed into his brain. He needed the sun—needed the light to beat back the memories invading his mind.

Gasping for air, he opened his eyes, tore his hat from his head, and raised his face toward the sun. The bright glare burned his irises, but he didn't care. He welcomed the burning of the rays that beat back the invasion. The pain was real, the pain was now, and the pain was the only damn thing to distract him from what he didn't want to remember.

A gentle touch on his forearm brought him back to the moment. He blinked several times to clear the flashing white spots from his eyes, and then glanced at Meg. Worry etched fine lines in her smooth-as-a-baby's-butt skin.

"Are you okay?" A shiver made her words tremble.

Pinching the bridge of his nose, he clamped his mouth shut and sucked in air through his nostrils. His heart still thundered like a herd of wild horses, but he'd strengthened his resolve enough to stand tall and face his sister. "I'm fine. You can't sneak up on a guy like that."

"I called your name, but you were staring off to God knows where." She squeezed his arm and then tucked a piece of hair behind her ear. "I'm sorry."

"My fault. I'm a little distracted."

Meg leaned to the side and glanced over his shoulder. "By the market?"

He swept a hand through the air and indicated the town square. "By everything. I haven't been back here for so long, and not one thing has changed. Hell, even the same lazy teenagers are lounging on the gazebo steps."

Meg's light eyebrows rose high on her head, and her lips quirked in a smirk. "Are you sure the town's distracting you and not Jillian?" She dipped her chin.

He spun as Jillian and Sam stepped out of the market. He moved his gaze along with Jillian down the street.

She rounded the corner and disappeared out of view.

The muscles in his stomach clenched. As awkward as facing Jillian again was, seeing her again had lit a spark inside of him—a spark he'd fight tooth and nail to ignite into the flame he craved. For the first time in a long time, he had hope for his future. Hope that would only grow once he had Jillian back.

Chapter Two

"Mom! Are you listening?" Sam's hurried pace never faltered as he spoke.

The rustling of the plastic bags hanging off her arm competed with the buzzing in her brain. She shook the cobwebs of confusion from her mind and glanced at Sam. "Sorry, honey. What did you say?"

"You should go to Jonah's party tonight." Sam leaned over and picked up a stick from the ground, never breaking his stride.

"I have too much to do. I need to finish plans for the new store, and concentrating on work will be easier when the house is quiet." Besides, seeing Jonah's soft blue eyes again was the last thing she needed right now. She'd spent years putting the pieces of her life back together after he'd abandoned her. She wouldn't throw away the peace she'd finally found for a stupid party.

Sam dragged the tip of the stick through the long blades of grass beside the sidewalk. "You work all the time."

The slight whine of his voice twisted her insides. The truth of his words stung. As a single parent, balancing her day was like swimming upstream with the world's strongest current beating her backward. She never got as far as she wanted and most days fell farther behind. Guilt was her constant companion. Guilt she wasn't enough for Sam. Guilt for missing out on important parts of his childhood. Guilt over every area of her life suffering because the day didn't contain enough hours to get everything done.

"How about I finish my work while you're gone so next week we can have the best last week of summer vacation ever?" The end of summer had snuck up, and she had a list of things to do before school started.

"As long as we don't have to go shopping." Sam slid a sideways glance.

She laughed and ran a hand through his tangled hair. His dark waves skimmed the nape of his neck and covered the tops of his ears. "No shopping as long as you get your hair cut." They turned onto the redbrick sidewalk stretched across her manicured yard and stopped at the oak stairs to her modest front porch. The soft creak of the rusted chains of her porch swing caught her attention, and she halted her footsteps. She placed a hand on the back of Sam's neck and slowed his pace.

Sam stood on his tiptoes and then broke loose and ran toward the house. "Dad!"

The creaking stopped, and Antonio stood with a crooked smile fixed on his handsome face.

The same dark curls she wanted cut from Sam's hair rested a little higher on Antonio's neck. The same dark eyes she stared into day after day now stared down with the identical hint of mischief that always lit Sam's irises.

Sam leaped onto the wooden porch and hurled himself into Antonio's arms.

A tug of tenderness pulled on her heart, just like it always did when their small, unconventional family was together. Pebbles crunched under her feet with every step toward them. "I didn't expect to see you for at least another hour and a half."

Antonio unwrapped himself from Sam and flashed a grin. Dimples sank at the corners of his mouth, and he tunneled his hand through his hair. "I planned on being here twenty minutes ago so technically I'm late."

"Some things never change." She shook her head, and the ends of her hair swayed across her back.

"And thank God for that." Antonio placed a kiss on the top of Sam's head and then steered him toward the front door. "Go get your stuff. I need to talk to your mom."

His words piqued her interest. Antonio never needed to talk to her alone. He was the fun parent who swooped in every couple of months for a boy's weekend or stopped in for a few hours when his flight schedule was slow. She was the parent who made all the decisions and actually raised their child. Antonio's sporadic appearances would drive most women crazy, but his inconsistent schedule worked for them.

Sam rounded his eyes. "Can't I hear?"

"No. Now, go on inside."

Antonio hardened his tone enough to broker no further argument, and Jillian blinked in surprise. Antonio never raised his voice, and Sam hurried inside. Jillian stepped onto the porch, rested a hip on the railing, and crossed both arms over her chest in her best tell-me-what-trouble-you're-in-now pose. "What's going on?" Antonio's chocolate eyes bore into hers.

"I want to move back to Smithview." He scrubbed a hand over the dark stubble that covered his olive skin and the lines in his forehead puckered.

The unexpectedness of his words knocked her off

balance, and she tightened her grip on the railing. The hard wood didn't help steady her. Her mind whipped in every direction like the leaves in the trees, and the smallest gust of wind threatened to topple her over the porch. "Why? You hated living here when we were married. Not much has changed in the last six years."

"I need to be around for Sam. Damn it, his childhood is almost over, and I've missed so much." A heavy sigh made his chest rise, and he dropped back down on the old swing. With his elbows on his knees, he hung his head in his hands. "I couldn't tell you the name of any of his teachers. I've never taken him to his first day of school. I'm a joke of a father."

She released her vise-like grip on the railing and sat beside Antonio. The soft cotton of his T-shirt nestled against her bare arm, and she laid a hand on the stiff fabric of his khaki shorts. "You're not a joke. Sam adores you, and he'd love to have you around more. I'm not sure why you sent him inside like a sad little puppy to tell me news that will make him so happy."

Antonio's hand covered hers.

Moisture gathered among the folds of her skin, but she faced her palm up and squeezed his hand instead of pulling away.

"So, it's okay if I move back?"

"Of course. Why wouldn't it be?"

He faced her, and the muscle above his eye twitched. "Because I don't want to just spend more time with Sam. I want to be here for you, too."

A high-pitched chuckle tickled her throat, and she focused on the nervous tick of his muscle he could never hide. The intensity of his gaze and the soft reverence in his words set her on edge. Good Lord, what exactly did he want? "If you see Sam more, I'll be around, too."

Antonio raised their joined hands and pressed his lips to her skin. "I want us to be a family again, Jillian. I want to give us another try."

A shiver shot through her hand, up her arm, and then down her spine. A shiver of excitement? A shiver of fear? Her mind shook from information overload. First Jonah and now Antonio. Breaking contact, she stared at the spot on her hand where the brand of his kiss lingered.

"Is that a no?"

His voice lowered an octave and vibrated her eardrum. "I...I don't know. What you're telling me is a lot to take in. I need to think."

"I understand. I've thought about us for a long time. I'll give you all the space you need. Just know I'm serious, Jillian. I want to be a family again more than anything." Antonio used his long legs to push the swing back and forth. The creak of the swing cut through the silence, and the wheels in her mind spun like a drunken college girl doing cartwheels—clumsy and unpredictable. Panic closed her throat. She and Antonio had a good system. Sure, she shouldered more responsibilities, but she also got to call all the shots.

Did she love Antonio? Had she ever loved him the same way she had once loved Jonah? Guilt burrowed into the lining of her stomach. One night close to nine years ago, she'd confided in a close friend to get over an old love and ended up with a child. Sam was her whole world and deserved a life with both of his parents.

The screen door squeaked open, and Sam popped

his head through the narrow space. "Can I come out now?"

At the interruption, she sagged in relief. Sliding away from Antonio, she patted the now-empty space between them. "Have a seat."

The swing dipped under the added weight, and Sam snuggled between them.

The smell of his coconut shampoo and the deodorant he now insisted on wearing surrounded him like a cloud of musk swirled through the air, in through her nose, and squeezed her heart.

"What were you talking about?" He pumped his legs back and forth.

The sudden motion messed with Jillian's equilibrium. She braced her feet on the wooden planks to stop the swinging. "Your dad has some big news." She turned toward Antonio and raised her brows.

Sam faced Antonio.

"I'm moving to Smithview."

"Really? I can't wait!" Sam jumped into Antonio's lap and wrapped his arms around his neck.

The eight-year-old boy who lingered on the edge of puberty left for a brief second, and the little boy who yearned for his father sat in his place. She pictured the three of them together sitting on the little porch in the pretty white house—the mom, the son, and the dad.

But even in the perfect family photo in her mind, she couldn't deny the lingering shadow of doubt in the corner of the frame. A shadow with a baseball hat pulled low over his face and combat boots on his feet. A shadow who called to her the way one no else ever had. A shadow who abandoned her in her darkest hour.

She lifted her gaze to the man beside her and

frowned.

And yet, Antonio had done the same thing.
****

Every groan, every shift, and every stab of longing echoed through her empty house after Sam left. She hated being home alone. Wandering through the rooms, she trailed her fingers along the walnut sofa table to check for dust, tidied a cluster of stray papers on the butcher block island in the kitchen, and checked on the laundry. Nothing needed doing. Nothing needed taking care of.

Tears clogged her throat, suffocating her like the loneliness keeping her hostage. She had to get out of here. A glint of silver on the granite countertop caught her eye. Car keys. Without considering where to go, she grabbed the keys and her purse and left the depression of a kid-free house.

She drove out of town and away from the craziness of the day, escaping the reminders of her encounter with Jonah and her talk with Antonio. The country road spread in front of her without a car in sight. Green stalks of corn towered along both sides of the road, the ears full and the silk beneath the husks turning brown. Her muscle memory took control of the wheel. The rows of corn split open like the mouth of Aladdin's cave and beckoned her toward a hidden oasis.

She turned into a deserted lot and parked under the shade of a weeping willow. With the car turned off, she leaned her forehead against the steering wheel and choked out a laugh. What sick part of her twisted brain led her to the dam? Memories of a simpler time assaulted her jumbled mind.

A soft melody drifted from her purse on the

passenger seat. She shifted her fingers around the hundred items no sane person needed in her purse until she found her phone. She glanced at the screen before answering the call.

"Hi, Mom. What's up?" She propped her elbow on the door and leaned her head on her hand.

"Hi, honey. I wanted to call and make sure Sam got off okay."

Her mom's voice was soft and gentle. Jillian smiled, pulled the keys out of the ignition, and stepped onto the hard pavement. Waves of heat shimmered off the blacktop. "They left fifteen minutes ago."

"Do you want me to come over?"

"Thanks for the offer, but I'm not home. I wanted to get out and enjoy the sunshine." She locked the car and took two steps before she remembered a book she'd been dying to read in her trunk. She pushed the button on her key fob to open the trunk and set the keys inside to search for the book underneath the reusable grocery bags.

"How nice. Are you out for a walk somewhere?"

"I'm at the dam."

Silence hung heavy on the line, and Jillian cringed. Her mom was aware of the time she'd spent here with Jonah.

"The dam's a strange place to go. You haven't been there in years."

Her words were tight, as if she struggled to get them out. Jillian placed the book under her arm and pinched the bridge of her nose. She didn't want to get into an argument. She used her free hand to close the trunk. The heavy thud vibrated through the trees and sent the birds fleeing toward the blue sky. "I wanted to be somewhere no one would bother me." She took a step away from the car, and dread pooled in her stomach like a ball of lead. "Oh no!"

"What's wrong? What's happening?"

Her mom's voice grew frantic. "I locked my keys in the trunk. I can't believe I did that. And I can't call the auto club because I let my membership expire."

"Do you have a spare key at the house?"

She heaved a heavy sigh and her mind raced as she tried to remember where her spare set of keys were, but every thought in her mind crawled through the muck of the past two hours. "Yeah, somewhere."

"I'll head to your place and find the key. Sit and read your book until I get there."

"Thanks, Mom." Jillian disconnected and glanced around. The weeping leaves dripped from the willow tree and offered welcomed shade from the blistering heat. She sat in front of the tree, and a slight curve in the rough trunk nestled against her back. Stretching out her legs, she opened her book to page one.

The words on the pages pulled at her to follow them down the rabbit hole. She tried to concentrate and lose herself in the story, but it was useless. One glance at her watch showed she had been on the first page for twenty minutes.

She placed the book on her lap and closed her eyes then ran her fingers through the blades of grass at her side. They tickled her palm, and she smiled. The same blades of grass used to tickle her flesh as she had lain beneath Jonah. The dim roar of the water flowing over the dam and into the stream below echoed in her ears. She could almost hear the way Jonah said her name with the same roar ringing loudly when they'd sit on the water's edge.

"Jillian."

She opened her eyes, and her breath caught. Chiseled calves that led to hard thighs and a narrow waist filled her vision. The light breeze caused his loose T-shirt to cling to his stomach, displaying the definition in his abs. She gulped and peered at his face. The shade from the bill of his hat hid his strong cheekbones and deep blue eyes, but his full lips were in plain view. She wet the top of her lip with her tongue before she tucked her bottom lip into her teeth.

How was having this reaction possible after everything that had happened?

Clearing her throat, she jumped to her feet and folded her arms across her chest. The quick, jerky movement caused her book to spill onto the grass. The urge to glance down seized her, but she fought the impulse and kept her gaze glued to his amused one.

His lip hitched in a smirk.

"What are you doing here?" She scowled. Her blood raced through her veins. Only she would be unlucky enough to see him twice in one afternoon.

He rubbed his jaw line and shifted his weight. "I wanted some quiet before heading to my mom's. The dam came to mind. Are you picking up your book?" He nodded toward the ground.

She didn't move.

He leaned forward and picked it up, extending his arm toward her.

Irritation swelled her veins. She grabbed the book, and her fingers brushed against his. Electricity coursed through her, and her heart thundered in her chest as quick as the water flowed down the dam. She clutched the book to her chest like a shield. "Thanks."

Jonah pulled back his hand and rubbed the bill of his hat. "No problem. Do you come here often?"

"I haven't been here in a long time." Nostalgia swam around her, and she bit her cheek to keep her emotions in check. The last thing she needed was for Jonah to see how much he affected her.

Jonah put his hands in his pockets and rocked back on his heels. "Still looks like a good spot to get away from the world."

"I guess so. I don't want to keep you from your quiet. I'll see you around." She hurried to her car then froze, her hand lingering on the handle.

"Is everything okay?"

A groan stalled in her throat. She needed to get away from Jonah. Where the hell was her mom? "It's fine. I'm waiting for my mom to get here with my keys."

He chuckled. "Lock your keys in the car? You being stranded in a parking lot outside your car brings back memories."

She snapped up her head, and her gaze bore into his. "I don't want to reminisce about old memories right now."

He stepped forward. "I'm sorry, Jilly. I didn't mean anything."

Closing her eyes, she took a long breath through her nose and fought like hell to keep her tears at bay. She opened her eyes again and cursed when moisture gathered in their corners. "I told you not to call me Jilly."

His shoulders hunched forward, and the corners of his mouth dipped. "Please, Jillian. Can't we talk about what happened?"

"Nothing you say will make things right."

Jonah pressed closer and lifted his chin.

The features once hidden by his hat came in to view. Confusion clouded his eyes, causing an inky darkness to overtake his baby blues.

"There's nothing I can say? What do you mean?"

Anger flared inside her. "You're a smart guy, Jonah. I shouldn't have to spell it out."

A car drove into the parking lot and parked beside her. Her mom peered over the steering wheel with wide eyes and lips pressed in a firm, no-nonsense line.

The passenger window slid open, and Pamela leaned over with keys dangling from her closed fist. "Honey, I have your keys."

Thank God. She grabbed the keys. "Thanks, Mom."

Her mom gave a small nod and pulled out of the parking lot.

Jillian put the spare key in the slot, and her hand shook. She opened the door and stood with a hand wrapped around the warm edge of the handle—needing to go but some part of her unwilling to leave.

"Will you come to my party tonight?"

He hurled the words like a Hail Mary pass to the end zone—quickly and with false hope.

"Why in hell would I go to your party?"

He shrugged and smiled. "To see Emma? She's bringing the kids. And my mom would be happy to see you. I'd be happy to see you."

Ignoring the boyish smile she'd fallen in love with, she shook her head and climbed into the car. Sweat made her hands slippery as she gripped the wheel and drove away. Jonah's reflection stared after her in the rearview mirror and was a sharp reminder of everything she'd lost. Nothing could be gained by letting down her guard. She couldn't risk a third encounter with Jonah today. She couldn't handle it.

Adjusting her rearview mirror, Jonah shrank into the distance and she focused on the open road in front of her. Or could she?

Chapter Three

"She's out of her mind," Jonah mumbled under his breath. A slight tremor took over his hands, and he bounced his knee up and down. The keys dangling from the ignition collided against his skin with every bounce.

The old truck jostled up and down over the uneven stones behind the barn. If he couldn't keep away from the horde of people at his mom's house, at least he could park away from the bumper-to-bumper parking littering the road so he could make a quick getaway. No one would notice him slinking into the shadows the trees along the property line provided.

The noise of the party muffled the groan of his door creaking open. His hunk of junk truck had been with him since before he'd left town. The rusted red paint and dented fender hid the excellent condition of the engine under the hood—the opposite of its owner. He was a chiseled soldier wearing a well-honed mask to hide the mess of a man he'd become.

If only he could make sure the mask didn't slip.

He weaved down the narrow path between his mom's house and the barn toward the front of the house and away from the music and laughter waiting in the backyard. Before he stepped into the lion's den, he needed a minute to collect himself. Fireflies sparkled in the evening sky, and he closed his eyes to let the sound of the singing cicadas calm his jangled nerves.

"Dude, what are you doing? Meditating?"

The deep timber of the voice behind him calmed him more than any damn cicadas. A shoulder brushed against him, and Jonah grinned. "Nah. Meditation doesn't work."

"Don't I know it."

Jonah nodded. Dylan knew. His best friend had spent four years in Iraq fighting side-by-side with the rest of their brothers in the Marine Corps. He hadn't taken long to realize he'd rather man a tractor on his family's farm instead of an assault rifle. Dylan had spent much more time fighting the demons he'd carried home.

Opening his eyes, Jonah took in the sight of the house he'd grown up in, and an ache pulsed in his chest. The farmhouse had gone through many transformations over the years; most of the changes came after his father died. The sudden hole in their lives had not only left them without a father, but the farm without a farmer. Needing to provide for three small children, his mom sold the farmland and transformed their home into an inn. Five acres remained, and she'd since added a nursery and horse stables to the property.

"How's it being home?"

"Weird." Jonah stepped to the porch stairs and ran his hand along the railing, stopping when his fingers found the notch with his and Jillian's initials. The pad of his finger rubbed over the indent, and he swept his gaze over the rest of the porch. His mom's favorite wicker chairs with a table in between sat on one side and the swing where he and Jillian shared their first kiss on the other.

The swing he'd sat on and waited for her to tell him good-bye before he'd left for boot camp.

The swing where his heart had been torn to shreds.

Shaking his head, he inhaled a deep breath and cleared the memories from his mind. He'd come back for Jillian, and rehashing their past was a waste of time. Worse things had happened since then. Things he couldn't get past without her by his side. "I can't believe my mom put a party together. All I want is to see my family. I can't deal with a party." He thrust his open palm toward the back of the house where every citizen of Smithview waited.

"Everyone's excited you're home. The prodigal son. The hometown hero. The...hell, I can't think of another stupid cliché for you."

Dylan rubbed his fingers along the thick, red beard on his chin, as if emulating the Thinking Man pose would bring another lame description to mind. Jonah chuckled. "How about the returning soldier who saw too much? The returning solider suffering from Post-Traumatic Stress Disorder who now has to deal with a party?" Nerves swirled in the pit of his stomach like soda shook in a can. Steadily building momentum until someone popped the top and the liquid exploded.

"You got this." Dylan clamped down his hand on Jonah's shoulder. "Go see Emma. She's in the kitchen with Meg. I'll meet you in the back."

Jonah sucked in a breath and stepped through the front door. He paused a moment in the foyer before heading down the narrow hall, passed the living room, and into the heart of his mother's home.

Meg glanced up from chopping tomatoes at the oversized island in the middle of the room.

"Mom will be mad you didn't go straight to the backyard." Meg quirked an eyebrow before getting back to her tomatoes.

Jonah rolled his eyes. "She's crazy, right? What the hell was she thinking?"

Emma glanced over her shoulder and then slid a casserole out of the oven. "Yes, she's crazy. But she's also over the moon her baby boy is home for good, and she can stop worrying. You being away hasn't been easy for her, you know."

"Can't I get a hello before you start the lecture?" He grinned and studied the shorter hair cut she'd finally opted for. He hadn't gotten a chance to visit his sister in Cleveland since his nephew was born a few months ago.

"I can do you one better." Emma put the casserole on the counter before throwing her arms around him. "I'm so happy to see you."

"I'm glad to see you, too." He hugged her tight, and the top of her head didn't even reach his chin. "Where are the kids?"

"You can't even give me two minutes before looking for the kids?" Emma placed both hands on her hips, and the waves in her light brown hair swayed around her heart-shaped face.

Jonah laughed, and the coil of tension around his neck loosened a little. "I guess old habits die hard for all of us."

"Sophie's outside with Luke, and I think Anderson's being passed around by every woman whose ovaries are crying out for more babies." Meg pointed toward the door with the sharp edge of the knife she'd used on the tomatoes.

Emma chuckled. "Wait until he starts screaming. No one's ovaries will make demands then."

"Can we stop talking about ovaries?" He appreciated the hell out of a woman's body, but some things he preferred not to picture.

"Sure we can because you need to get outside. Please put a smile on your handsome face, and act like you're a little happy to see everyone," Emma said.

He grimaced.

Meg laughed.

Just like when they were kids, Meg, the youngest of the three, loved when he found himself in an awkward situation. If only she understood how bad things really were.

Meg arranged the sliced tomatoes on a plate and glanced at him. "I'm glad the party's for you and not me. Be a good little boy and listen to mommy number two."

Emma passed behind Meg and slapped her on the back of her head on the way to the door. She pushed it open and pasted a sweet-as-sin smile on her face. "After you."

Jonah groaned and stepped beside his sister, hoping to gain a few more moments before he entered hell.

"You can put up with a little party, Jonah. Give her an hour. Sit down, eat some food, and then you can escape with Sophie to the barn. Who knows, you might even enjoy catching up with some old friends."

She was right. Damn it, Emma usually was. He stepped onto the large deck and studied the expansive yard. People scattered around the white-washed deck, eating and talking amongst themselves. He hurried down to the yard, and no one glanced his way. He breathed deeply, and a weight settled on his shoulders. Casting his gaze toward the ground, he slumped his shoulders forward and searched for his mom.

She stood with a group of women from the church under a giant oak tree, who fussed over a cooing Anderson.

Sophie spied him and squealed from her perch on the tire swing. "Uncle Jonah!"

His heart pounded at the sound of his name. Heads twisted in his direction. A dozen voices rang out and welcomed him home. Hands patted his back, and each touch landed like a bullet. He kept his gaze focused on Sophie, still swinging on the tire.

Her dad scooped her off, and the little girl ran toward him.

Luke lifted a hand in greeting, his smile wide as he watched Sophie fly across the yard.

His brother-in-law had acquired black-framed glasses since the last time he'd seen him. Jonah made a mental note to give him a hard time about getting old when he circled back. He crouched to the ground and opened his arms wide.

She hurled herself into his body.

He buried his face in her neck and breathed in the scent of baby shampoo and sweat. "Hi there, baby girl. How are you?" He didn't register the words pouring from her mouth. The blood pulsed too loudly in his ears to hear anything. He kept his gaze locked on her cherub face. He focused on the wisps of blonde hair that slipped from her pigtails and the way her blue eyes sparked when she spoke. The more she talked, the calmer he became. He stood with her in his arms. Steadier now, he made his way to his mom.

"How the hell did you sneak out here without anyone noticing?" Annie pressed her lips into a pout.

Disappointment clouded her eyes. She'd traded in her overalls for a pretty summer dress that flowed with the subtle breeze. Her dyed-blonde hair hung in soft curls around her face, the artificial color matching Meg's strand for strand. But her sapphire blue eyes and petite frame were a dead ringer for what Emma would look like in twenty-five years. "Sorry. I wanted a second to say hi to Emma before the craziness started." The lie dripped from his tongue.

"Oh, I guess I can understand you wanting to say hi to your sister." Annie held up the baby in her arms. "Did you get a chance to meet your nephew yet?"

Jonah glanced at the light-haired baby. "He's cute."

"Not as cute as me," Sophie said.

"He's a different kind of cute, sweetheart." Annie suppressed a smile. "Do you want to hold him, Jonah?"

Jonah narrowed his gaze on his nephew. "I'll stick to Sophie. He's pretty content with you for the moment."

Sophie smooshed his cheeks between her chubby hands. "Yeah, stick with me."

"You can keep Sophie close, but make sure you mingle a little bit. A lot of folks want to talk to you. Isn't it nice they all showed up?"

Jonah swallowed a groan and then forced a smile. "Very. Thanks for the party, Mom." He visited with Sophie until the traitor dumped him for Meg. With her gone, he couldn't stand quietly while she took over the conversation. Somehow, he mustered the strength to keep going, even though his anxiety ricocheted off his ribs like a bouncy ball. Every step he took led to more slaps on the back. Every touch made his insides itch. Too many faces crowded his vision. Hell, he didn't recognize half these people.

Why would they even come? He was a spectacle to them, some kind of war specimen everyone wanted to touch. His heart shivered in his chest with rapid palpitations. Sweat collected on the top of his upper lip, and he wiped it away with the back of his hand. Laughter boomed around him like a grenade, and he summoned maximum effort not to cover his ears.

He spun in a circle and searched for a path of escape. He needed to get out of here. Turning toward the barn, he took a step toward freedom, frantic to be alone.

"Hey, big guy. Good to have you back in town."

Meg's idiot fiancé, Blake, stepped in front of him and blocked his path. His wide grin oozed fake charm. Hell, he wouldn't be surprised if Blake paid for the highlights in his sandy brown hair. Jonah bit into the soft flesh of his cheek to keep from groaning. He'd only met Blake a few times when the family had gathered at Emma's, and every time he liked the guy less. Meg deserved better. "Thanks." He lowered his gaze to the ground and tried to pass Blake. Sweat saturated the underarms of his T-shirt, and his heart beat a rapid rhythm. He clutched his chest, and the thin material of his shirt bunched in his hand.

"You leaving?" Blake side-stepped again.

The alcohol on Blake's breath mixed with the humid air and hit Jonah in the face like a dirty, wet towel. "Yeah. Do you mind?" He ground the words through clenched teeth and lifted his head to stare into Blake's amused gaze.

Blake threw his hands in the air in an I-didn't-do-anything gesture and smirked but didn't get out of the way. "I wanted a chance to get to know you a little better. Chill."

Jonah ran his tongue over his top row of teeth and swallowed the anger churning up his esophagus. He curled his hands into fists of fury at his sides. "Maybe later. Now, get out of my way."

"What's your problem?"

The golden boy veneer slipped, and Blake's true colors shimmered from his taut muscles.

Jonah lowered a shoulder and shoved by him. A hard tug of his shirt had him stumbling backward. He spun a slow semi-circle, and a growl clawed its way from his throat. "Knock it off."

Blake's laugh caught the attention of clusters of people around them. "I'm messing with you. Take it easy, soldier boy."

His words were meant as a taunt, but Jonah wouldn't take the bait. He couldn't.

People moved toward them and boxed him into an invisible cage. The added attention had the hairs on the back of his neck standing at attention. Every gaze fixed on him was like a needle sticking into his skin. He dug his fingernails into the palms of his hands until his short nails pierced his flesh. But he kept digging so he wouldn't put his fist into Blake's smug face. "I'll tell you one more time. Get out of my way."

Blake took a step forward, and the gathering crowd pushed in closer.

The smell of cheap beer wafted up Jonah's nose, and nausea pitched in his stomach, but he stood his ground.

"What will you do about it? Shoot me?"

Blake lowered his voice so the words stayed between them. Jonah's fists shook, and his breath puffed out in short, quick spurts. His heartbeat hammered against his chest like a prisoner wanting to break free from his cage. Moisture pooled at the base of his neck, and he shut his eyes to fight against the ringing in his head. The heat of a hundred gazes burned through him. He couldn't lose it now. He had to get away.

Another harsh laugh grumbled from Blake's mouth. "What's wrong with you?"

So much was wrong. So much had happened nobody knew about. Images flashed through his mind. Blood, fire, and death blended together, and the smell of burning flesh invaded his senses. He opened his eyes and voices rose louder and pushed his nerves to the edge of a cliff he couldn't jump from or he couldn't turn back.

He stepped back and swept his gaze over the yard for a comforting face. But all the faces blurred, and panic froze his blood. His nerves stretched tighter like a stretched rubber band—taut and ready to snap. He glanced in front of him, praying to God Blake would step out of the way and let him pass without causing more of a scene.

"You're crazy." Blake snorted and shook his head.

And the rubber band broke. A low, guttural yell vibrated from Jonah's gut, and he lunged, driving Blake to the ground.

Screams of shock echoed around him

He didn't care. He pulled back his arm and sent his fist into the hard line of Blake's jaw.

"Jonah!"

In the corner of his mind, he registered his mom's voice, but he couldn't stop. He'd been pushed too far. He landed another punch on Blake's mouth, and the force of the hit sent shivers of pain up his arm. He pulled back his fist again, but a gentle touch on his elbow had him turning his head. His gaze landed on a pair of calming green eyes. The same eyes that had saved him once before. A whoosh of air from his lungs left him deflated. Jillian's hand skimmed down his forearm, and she intertwined her fingers with his.

"Come on, Jonah. Let's go for a walk."

Chapter Four

Jillian yanked Jonah to his feet. He clung to her hand like a lifeline. His fingertips crushed her knuckles and sent a beat of apprehension against her skin.

"Jonah!" Annie ran up beside them and cradled his face in her hands. "Are you okay?"

He didn't respond or tear his gaze from her to even acknowledge his mom. Panic darkened the blue of his eyes to black.

"I've got him, Annie." Jillian spared the older woman a quick glance. Her heart ached from the helplessness in Annie's eyes and the lines of worry etched across her forehead. A mother had an undying need to protect her child, but Jonah didn't need his mom right now.

Blake scrambled off the ground. He brushed dirt from the back of his pants, and it flew into the night air. Blood trickled from the corner of his mouth, and he wiped it off with the back of his hand.

Sadness and confusion and anger all mixed together and shone from Jonah's eyes. Jillian locked her gaze on his and ignored the jumbled slurs spewing from Blake's mouth. Responding to Blake was the last thing Jonah needed. He needed calmness and reassurance, and God help her, he needed her.

"Is anyone doing anything? You all saw him. He attacked me." Blake turned in a circle and shouted at the people standing around them, gawking at the spectacle.

"What's going on?" Meg shoved her way through the crowd. "What's wrong?"

"Your brother coldcocked me for no damn reason."

"Watch your mouth, Blake." Annie drew in a shaky breath, and red stained her cheeks. "I don't know what happened, but I won't have you speaking rudely about my son."

Meg's wide eyes glanced at Jillian.

She shook her head to deflect any questions. "I need to get Jonah away from here. Deal with Blake." She couldn't help the disgust that coated her words. She'd witnessed the whole exchange between the two, and if she'd gotten to Blake first, she would have done a whole lot worse than a fist to the face.

Jillian squared her shoulders and led Jonah away from the chaos. Her mind spun faster with every wedged footstep that sank into the soft grass. What was she supposed to say? She'd come here tonight to prove he didn't have any pull over her and he meant nothing to her. Hell, she hadn't even planned to speak to him.

But she couldn't prevent her gaze from seeking him out the entire evening. When panic had etched itself on his face, she'd had no choice but to jump in. Even if she had no idea how to help.

The farther away from the crowd they got, the stronger Jonah's grip became. Instead of her leading him, he fell into step beside her. The warmth of his body next to hers calmed the adrenaline coursing through her veins. The warmth of his hand in hers heated her blood and flooded her with memories. Years and distance stretched between them, but somehow, his hand fit into hers the way it always had. His fingers entwined with hers like a missing puzzle piece completing her.

They stopped at the split-rail fence corralling in the horses, and Jillian dropped his hand. Jonah, this place, the touch of his hand…everything was all too much. She leaned her elbows on the top of the fence and stared into the pasture. Darkness wrapped around them like a shield and protected them from the din dying down over their shoulders. The outlines of the horses dotted the landscape, and the subtle summer breeze whispered against her face, cooling the flames of turmoil inside her.

Jonah leaned against the wooden plank beside her, and it wiggled with his weight. Engines purred to life, and headlights cut through the darkness. The party was over.

She studied his profile. The contorted lines from earlier had smoothed, and his short brown hair rebelled against the military-issued buzz cut. He focused his gaze in front of him, intent on either the horses in the field or the horror in his mind. She didn't ask which, because she feared the answer. The sudden swivel of his head toward her caught her off guard, and heat flooded her cheeks.

A huff of air puffed from Jonah's mouth.

He'd caught her staring.

He lifted the side of his mouth, and his hooded eyes narrowed on her.

She stiffened her spine to fight the urge to flatten the wrinkles on her tank top. Instead, she collected her hair at the nape of her neck and then shifted it over her shoulder, moving her fingers through the strands.

Jonah's lips tilted into the first smile he'd shown all night. "I've missed the hell out of you, Jilly."

She let the nickname roll over her like a cashmere throw—warm, familiar, and comfortable. The tenderness in his voice melted the outer layer of her resentment. "I've missed you, too." His vulnerability had her confiding the truth before she could stop the words from leaving her mouth.

He straightened and leaned toward her.

This close, she could make out the puckered skin on his brow and a light scar trailing down his cheek. A scar his hat had hidden before. She lifted a hand and grazed the tip of her finger along the raised skin. "Are you okay?"

He closed his eyes and took a deep breath. His hand covered hers and trapped it against his face. He opened his eyes, and unshed tears clung to his lashes. "No, but I will be. Now that I'm here. Now that you're close."

The intensity of his words made her break eye contact and put a little distance between them. She hooked the toe of her shoe in the bottom rail of the fence and stared into the darkness. She came to the party to prove he didn't mean anything to her, not pick up the pieces of their broken relationship. "Jonah, I was helping you get away from Blake. I didn't forget everything that happened between us."

"We'll never forget, but why can't we move forward? I've spent every day for the past twelve years regretting the way things ended. Regretting I wasn't the man you needed. You not showing up the day I left hurt like hell, but I'm willing to let that incident go. You were young and didn't know how to tell me I wasn't a good enough man."

His words left her breathless, and she reared back her head as if he'd slapped her. She wished he had. The pain of his palm to her cheek would have hurt less. "You assumed I didn't show up to say good-bye because I thought I was better than you?" She hated the way her voice trembled, but damn it, she couldn't stop it.

"Why else wouldn't you have come?" Lines creased in the corners of his eyes.

Her jaw dropped. "So, the only reason I wouldn't have shown up is because I was a spoiled brat?" Anger blazed a hole in her stomach. Twelve years of hurt crashed down on her like ice water. "You know damn well why I wasn't there."

"But I—"

She held up a hand. After years of pining for an apology, she didn't want to hear another word out of his mouth. "I was wrong to come here. I thought the more I saw you, the easier it would be. I need to stay away. Seeing you does nothing but make me mad and remind me of everything I lost." She pushed off the fence and turned toward the house.

Jonah grabbed her wrist.

She spun and yanked her arm from his grasp. "Don't touch me." She stalked toward her car, and the unruly blades of grass tickled her ankles. She'd been an idiot for coming, but at least now she could move forward and focus on her future—a future without Jonah Sheffield.

****

On Sunday morning, Jillian sat with her feet curled under her and her favorite wool blanket draped over her shoulders. Soft cushions hugged her close in her oversized armchair, but her muscles still bunched together on high alert. The book she'd started reading two days before sat on her lap. Seconds passed into minutes which stretched into hours, and page one laid before her and taunted her inability to make it past one damn page.

She sent a mental apology to Ms. Keith and closed the romantic suspense she'd been dying to read. Nothing could pull her mind from the events of the past few days. Not even her favorite writer.

The frantic rustling from the front doorknob caught her attention, and she searched for the clock on the mantel.

Sam.

Tossing the blanket and book to the floor, she ran to the door and threw it open.

Sam stood in the doorway with Antonio behind him.

The glare of the afternoon sun shined through the open door. The golden rays and the smile of her little boy chased away the cloud of gloom hovering over her head. "Come here, little man."

Sam ran into her arms and knocked her back onto the tile floor in the foyer.

Jillian retaliated by tickling the tender flesh of his sides. Squeals of laughter chased the quietness from her home.

Sam rolled to his back, but the large bookbag attached to his shoulders weighed him down like a sack of bricks.

Or a sack of books, in the case of her little bookworm.

"You look like a turtle flailing around on the floor." Antonio chuckled. He stepped over the tangled pile of limbs and tossed Sam's overnight bag in the corner.

Jillian stood and then helped Sam to his feet. "Did you two have fun?"

"I rode the tallest roller coaster. It was awesome!" Enthusiasm rang from every word.

The tallest roller coaster at Cedar's Edge was one of the fastest in the world. A shudder climbed up her spine the way the roller coaster Sam rode climbed the first hill. No way she'd have let him ride the Rapid Falcon, and she shot Antonio a look that conveyed exactly what she thought over Sam's head.

Antonio threw his palms in the air and hunched his shoulder to his ears. "Sorry, but I couldn't talk him out of it. Do you think I wanted to ride that death trap?"

"I remember going to the amusement park with you. You always talked me into riding every ride." She couldn't help but giggle at the memories of flying down the tall hills with the wind blowing in her face.

"And you loved every minute of it." Antonio flashed his dimples.

The glare she gave him didn't fool him one bit. She pressed her lips together but couldn't quite keep the smile from her lips. "You might be right, but I'm glad I wasn't there to see Sam riding the roller coasters. I would have had a heart attack."

"You totally have to come next time, Mom." Sam's backpack fell to the floor with a soft thud, and he kicked the bag toward the wall.

Jillian lifted her brows. "Nice try, buddy. Please put your stuff in your room."

"Fine." Sam glanced at Antonio. "Are you leaving?"

"I don't have to, but it's up to your mom. She might have things to do. I don't want to intrude." Antonio's gaze found hers.

She wished she had an answer for all the questions in his eyes. He was like a lost puppy who didn't want to be sent away. Not now. Not ever. "No plans. Stay as long as you'd like."

"Sweet! I'll be right back." Sam scooped his backpack off the floor, grabbed the overnight bag Antonio dropped, and ran down the hall.

Antonio's shoulders sagged, and his wide smile showed off a straight, white line of teeth.

"How about some coffee?" Jillian made a beeline to the coffee machine on the countertop. Not knowing how long Antonio would stay, she filled the pot to the top with water before dumping it into the machine and grabbing the ground coffee from the cabinet.

Antonio took a seat on one of the two stools at the breakfast bar. "What did you do over the weekend? Did you get together with Catie?"

Coffee grounds spilled from the plastic scoop and scattered on the floor. His casual question set her nerves atwitter. She couldn't tell him about her evening at the inn for Jonah's welcome home party. She'd told Antonio about her past with Jonah—all of it. If she told him Jonah was back in town and she'd gone to his mother's house to welcome him home, she was unsure of Antonio's reaction. Better not to mention it. "No, I didn't get a chance to see Catie. I got some work done. Construction on the space I bought above Kiddy Korner begins tomorrow. I'm turning it into another bookstore.

41

Kiddy Korner has done so well, and I want to bring something to town to benefit everybody." She bent over to scrape the grounds into the palm of her hand. Her gray cotton shorts inched up the backs of her thighs, and she cringed.

God, I hope he doesn't think I'm showing him my backside. She straightened too fast, and the brown grainy grounds spilled back on the floor. "Shoot." Antonio's soft chuckle grazed the back of her neck like the first tender touch of a tentative lover—sweet, affectionate, and just a little bit awkward.

"Having trouble?" He nodded toward the floor.

She wiped the grounds to the side with her foot. Stray bits clung to her skin, and she wiped the bottom of her bare foot on top of the other to scrape them off. "I'll get them later." She spared him a sidewise glance, and the amusement on his face brought heat to her cheeks. This weird awareness of Antonio was new. Not an awareness of him as the father of her child or the ex-husband who'd always been her friend, but as a man who wanted to be with her. Heavy footsteps fell against the floor like a herd of elephants stampeding.

Sam slid on his white socks into the kitchen. "Can we watch a movie?"

"As long as it's not the one with the blocks." Jillian grabbed two mugs from the dishwasher she hadn't gotten around to emptying.

Sam yanked open the refrigerator door and grabbed a juice box. "Oh man. Why not?"

The subtle whine in his words worked her nerves.

Funny how two short days had made her forget the little things about her son that could send her on a tailspin of annoyance. Funnier still how she wouldn't change it for the world. "Because I've seen it twenty times in the last month. How about we compromise? We watch the new dragon movie, and I'll make popcorn." Sam's wide grin showed the crooked front tooth that would no doubt lead him to braces soon.

"Deal."

"You two set up the movie, and I'll be in the living room in a minute."

Antonio hopped off the stool and placed an arm around Sam's shoulders as they hurried into the living room.

They made a handsome pair—one tall and broad and full of Latino charm and one lanky and lean and full of the goodness only a child could possess. They were her family, and nothing would ever change that. But could their dynamic shift? If she decided to give Antonio another chance, their family could grow stronger.

Or giving Antonio another chance could ruin everything she'd worked so hard to hold together.

Chapter Five

Chaos reigned in the construction site. Loud cracks of drywall crumbling to the ground echoed around him and sent sparks of fire shooting from Jonah's nerve endings. Nervous energy zipped around his body and tried to break free, leaving him jumpy as hell. Chalky white debris circled in the air and coated everything in sight. Jonah tightened his grip around the handle of his hammer until the tough wood burned calluses into his hand.

Getting a job on a construction site might be the worst idea he'd ever had, but he didn't have much of a choice. Smithview didn't offer a lot of job opportunities outside of farming and family-run businesses. Unless he wanted to work with his mom tending to guests at the inn or planting flowers at the nursery, he needed to learn a new trade. Lack of jobs was the main reason Emma had moved across the state after she graduated from college. The move benefited him since his family would meet him in Cleveland for visits instead of making him drive the extra three hours to the northwest corner of Ohio.

The buzz of saws and screech of shouting coworkers grated on every pulse-pounding need to either curl in a ball in the corner or put his fist through the decaying wall in front of him. But neither reaction would help him cope with the reality of his new job. He should have known better.

Working on the construction crew put him close to Jillian. She couldn't avoid him if he worked at her bookstore, and being around her so much wouldn't allow her to avoid admitting how he made her feel. Her actions on Friday night had shown she was still drawn to him. Even if her words were a bit murkier.

Her anger toward him confused the hell out of him, but he'd get to the bottom of things. He had to.

"Watch out!"

A deep voice boomed the order. The whiskers above Jonah's top lip moistened with perspiration, and he fell to the ground face first, covering his head with his hands.

Soft snickers bounced off the high ceilings.

He lifted his head off the filthy floor.

An old fluorescent light swung on a thick cord in the middle of the room, and a few members of the crew glanced in his direction with smirks.

"You're fine, son. Get on up."

A pair of worn boots stepped into his line of vision. Jonah grabbed the hammer he'd dropped, jumped to his feet, and knocked the dirt and dust from his jeans. He kept his gaze lowered, not wanting to see his boss's reaction to his moment of stupidity. "Sorry 'bout that, Gus."

"Look at me, Jonah."

Gus's voice held the same don't-mess-with-me quality most of his commanding officers had possessed. Jonah drew in a deep breath, and the tiny specks of dirt in the air coated his throat. He lifted his head, set his jaw, and locked his gaze on the tired brown eyes of his old-as-dirt boss. "Yes, sir."

"You okay?"

Gus's soft words stood in stark contrast to his leathery skin and jowls that rivaled an old basset hound. "Yes, sir." Jonah dropped his hands to his sides.

The hum and hammering of the worksite morphed into creaking floorboards and whispered jokes.

"Best thing you can do is keep your mind and hands busy. Being home from war gets easier over time." Gus nodded toward the hammer dangling from his tight grasp. "Put that son of a gun through a wall. You'll never get a better chance to take out your aggression than demolition day. Hell, I'm even paying you to beat down these walls."

Jonah dipped his chin and quirked an eyebrow. "Sir?"

Gus gave a quick glance over his shoulder, but his expression was enough to get the jerks judging him back to work.

The noise picked up, but this time it soothed him. Well, soothe might be an exaggeration, but it didn't push him to the breaking point.

"I've been where you are. Fresh home from a war and finding my way. Vietnam. Had a hell of a hard time when I returned to civilian life." Gus ran a palm over his cheek. "But I figured it out, and you will too. For now, keep those hands working. Trust me, it helps."

Jonah dropped his gaze to the hammer. The tool hung heavy in his hands, and he swung it back and forth to test its weight—back and forth, back and forth. Each swing arched higher and faster. Each swing stirred the stifling air around his face. Each swing brought a sense of control and power over the demons clawing their way through his psyche.

A primitive grunt started deep in his gut and forced its way through his mouth. The sound mingled with the commotion around him. He lifted his arm above his head and slammed the head of the hammer into the drywall. He grunted louder, and the need to smash his hammer into something hard and unrelenting grew more frantic. He lifted his hand once more and connected the hammer with the wall. Splintered drywall flew around him, and the hole grew as he hit it again and again.

The head of the hammer wedged into a nook, and he yanked to set it free. His grip slipped, and he stumbled backward. His breath came out in short gasps, and he leaned forward to place his hands on his knees. Streams of sweat coursed down his face, and he let the beads of moisture fall—fall to the ground in tiny plops of freedom.

"Feel better?"

Jonah straightened and found himself once again face-to-face with his boss who he'd known most of his life. A hardened old man who had been to war and returned broken. But Gus had figured out his problems and gone on with his life. Jonah nodded. "Yes, sir."

"Good. Now keep going. I need this demo done quick." Gus gave him a slap on his shoulder and then left to get back to whatever he'd been doing.

Jonah lifted his gaze to the hammer still stuck in the wall. His hope lifted a fraction. Maybe he could do this after all.

The click-click-clack of heels against the subfloor cut through the noise.

Jonah twisted toward the sound, and his hopes rose even higher.

Jillian stood tall and proud in front of Gus with her hands moving in all directions. Her cream-colored skirt hugged the subtle curves of her backside, and the sleeveless blouse showed off toned arms.

Her head spun in his direction, and her eyes widened.

Their eyes locked for the briefest of seconds, and the rapid beats of his heart matched the pounding of a sledgehammer on the other side of the room.

She dropped her arms to her side, and her body stiffened. She faced Gus with no more frantic animation of limbs, and then stalked down the stairs.

So much for being in her face. If he wanted to be a thorn in her side, he'd have to find a way to dig a little deeper.

By the end of the workday, the stiff muscles in Jonah's neck screamed for relief. A hot shower, a good meal, and a comfortable bed waited. He couldn't get back to the little house he'd rented in the woods fast enough. He jumped into his truck and brought the engine to life.

Ping.

A text message signaled on his phone, and he swiped the touch screen to read the message.

—*Wanna grab a beer with me and D?*—

Pressure built between his eyes, and he leaned against the seat. He'd avoided Meg over the weekend, which hadn't been easy since they both wanted to spend time with Emma and the kids. They were polite, which was weird as hell, but never talked about Blake. Ignoring the tension had been like pretending a giant elephant with a bright pink tutu and a bedazzled hat wasn't in the room.

But he couldn't avoid her forever. Hell, he didn't want to. He moved his fingers over the phone's keyboard.

—*Sure. Be there in five*—

The Village Idiot was the only bar in town and sat on the opposite corner of Jillian's store. No need to ask Meg where to meet her and Dylan, and definitely no need to drive there. He cut the engine and climbed out of the truck. The summer sun barely lowered in the sky and still shot down enough heat to have him cursing the stiff jeans and work boots that forced his internal temperature higher. The heat didn't help with the smell of his sweat-soaked T-shirt either. Jonah hurried toward the bar.

Kids screaming their last-days-of-summer anthem ran up and down the sidewalks, popping in and out of stores along the square.

What he wouldn't give to go back to the carefree days of his youth. Even if he could only return for a day. He ran his fingers over the hair on the back of his head. Damn it, he should have grabbed his hat from his truck. The buzz cut he despised had grown into an in-between hair style he hated even more, but he refused to cut it. He refused to do anything he'd been forced to do while in the military.

A quick glance at the parking spots lining the street showed him both Meg and Dylan beat him here. He wrapped his fingers around the door handle to the bar, and the heated metal scorched his skin. After opening the door, he blinked to adjust to the lack of natural light inside.

Nostalgia washed over him. Just like most of the town, not much had changed. The same square tables littered most of the open space. The same pool tables sat at the back of the room. The same bartender stood behind the bar with a white towel draped over his shoulder.

Jonah huffed out a laugh. Good ol' Paul was as weathered as the wooden bar. Jonah couldn't count the number of times he'd tried to get Paul to sell him alcohol as an under-age kid. For the first time, he could take a seat at the bar and actually get served.

"Hey, Jonah," Dylan called from a stool at the far end of the long bar. Low lights hung from the ceiling, almost skimming the top of Dylan's head. "I ordered you a beer."

Meg sat beside him and hunched over a frosted mug.

Jonah ambled toward them and waved at Paul on his way to his seat. "Good to see you, Paul."

Paul nodded and grabbed the towel off his shoulder. "You too, Jonah. Good to have you home. First drink's on the house." He wiped a nonexistent spot from the bar.

Gratitude straightened Jonah's spine, and he took a seat on the empty stool next to Meg. Red splotches dotted her pale skin.

She lifted her mug and eyed him over the rim.

He mentally kicked himself for not talking to her sooner. "We okay?"

Meg nodded and took a sip from her mug before setting it back on the bar. "Yeah."

And with one word, the uneasiness between them melted away like a fine mist blowing out to sea. Nothing more needed to be said. If he fought with Emma, they'd need an entire conversation about how they felt. But not with Meg. God, he loved how low-maintenance she was.

"Well, ain't that sweet," Dylan said.

"Shut up." Jonah laughed at Dylan's fake Southern drawl and reached across Meg to grab the bottle of beer from in front of Dylan. The bitter taste of his favorite American ale relaxed the muscles in his neck a whole hell of a lot better than a hot shower. "What are you two doing together?"

Dylan's cheeks turned the same shade of red as his beard, and he glanced away.

Meg kept her gaze glued to her fingers tap-tap-tapping against the bar. "Dylan stopped by the inn to tell Emma, Luke, and the kids bye. When we noticed the time, we figured we'd see if you wanted to grab a drink."

"We wondered how your first day went," Dylan slapped a hand on Jonah's shoulder.

Jonah shrugged off Dylan's hand and peeled the moist label from his bottle. "My day was fine."

"Really? Everybody knows Gus can be a jerk, and all the noise must have driven you crazy." Meg lifted her gaze to meet his.

Meg's voice held more than a hint of doubt. "I'm not crazy." The bottle slipped from his hand and teetered to the side before landing back on its round bottom. Beer spilled from the top and splashed on the bar.

Meg winced. "I didn't mean *you're* crazy."

Jonah sighed and rubbed the back of his neck. "I know. I'm sorry. The noise was rough at first, but it got easier as the day progressed. I need to figure out how to channel what I'm feeling into what I'm doing. I think getting out my emotions with physical labor might help."

Meg chewed her bottom lip.

Good thing she wasn't one to wear lipstick or it would have coated her white teeth.

"Did you see Jillian?" she asked.

He hadn't spoken to anyone about his conversation with Jillian on Friday night. Hell, he hadn't spoken with anyone about his intentions toward her. Even though he'd be surprised if his family and Dylan hadn't figured it out. Judging by Meg's sudden interest in biting a hole through her lip, she wasn't happy about the idea of him winning back Jillian. "Just for a second. Why?"

Meg and Dylan glanced at each other with their lips quirked to the side.

Goose bumps erupted over his skin. His best friend and his baby sister being in cahoots didn't sit well.

Dylan cleared his throat. "What are your plans with her? Friday night she was the only one who could get through to you. Do you want to get back together?"

"What does it matter?" Jonah's words snapped out like a snapping turtle in the local creek—hard and unrelenting. His plans were nobody's business.

"Be careful." Meg turned toward him with wide blue eyes and winced.

The calmness of her voice and wariness in her eyes set him on edge. "What do you mean?"

Meg took a deep breath and slid her empty glass to the edge of the bar. "I was at the flower shop today, and I overheard Frida Johnson talking to Celeste about showing Antonio Mendez some houses this week."

"So?" The man's name held a hint of familiarity, but he couldn't place him. Jonah wasn't sure why he should care about a stranger's interest in buying real estate in Smithview.

"Antonio is Jillian's ex-husband. He shows up now and then to see their son, but he hasn't lived here since he and Jillian got divorced. Frida was going on and on about how he's searching for a nice family home."

Jonah's stomach dropped to the dirty floor. He'd planned on taking his time in showing Jillian he was a changed man who she could be proud to be with—a man who needed her. But if her ex-husband was back in town with the same intention, he needed to act faster. Shoving up from the bar, he grabbed his beer bottle and drained it. He needed to figure out where Jillian's head was. Determination strengthened his resolve. He couldn't lose her again.

Chapter Six

Jillian stood in the house Antonio considered buying and stared into the closet. She counted ten rolls of toilet paper, twenty pairs of women's shoes, and the most beautiful trench coat she'd ever seen. She itched to touch the luxe fabric. Designer labels made her knees weak and her bank account scream in agony. The high-end jacket in a stranger's house Antonio might buy called to her for one tiny touch, because God knew she'd never afford one of her own. She might be confused as to why Antonio wanted her to check out this house with him, but one touch of this fabulous coat would make the trip worth it.

"Must be one hell of a hall closet." Antonio stood behind her. "Ahh, I see what's caught your attention."

His breath tickled the back of her neck. Jillian chuckled, turned to face him, and collided with the hard muscles of his chest.

His hands clasped around her waist to steady her, and his fingertips grazed the small of her back.

She shimmied her shoulders in a tiny shudder and took a step back. "You caught me. I can't figure out the toilet paper in the hall closet. Shouldn't it be in the bathroom?"

The corner of Antonio's mouth hitched up. One hand stayed on her back and the other cupped her cheek. The pad of his thumb traced her cheekbone.

Desire burned in his chocolate colored eyes instead of amusement. Unable to break contact or invite him in for more, she swallowed hard.

Confusion clouded her consciousness. Antonio was a good man, even if he hadn't always been around. But part of his distance was her fault. She always clung to the all-consuming first love that had left her breathless and her heart full—a love that also left her shattered and barely clinging to life.

Antonio had breathed life into her in her darkest hour. He'd been there when she needed him most. But was Antonio helping her through a tough time, and the son they shared, enough to build a future on? Maybe the time had come to take off the rose-colored glasses in viewing her time with Jonah.

She took a step forward and leaned her cheek into Antonio's touch. A spark of surprise lightened his eyes.

"I wish I could read your mind," he whispered.

"Me, too. Maybe you'd have a better time figuring out what it's saying." She placed her hand on his chest and pressed against him.

He lowered his head, and his mouth hovered over hers.

She held her breath and waited for the moment of truth of what the touch of his lips would do to her body.

"This place is awesome!"

Thank God Sam's voice drifted into the hall before he did. She jumped away from Antonio and ran a hand over her ponytail. Relief, and a little bit of disappointment, pulsed in her veins.

Sam rounded the corner from the living room. "Dad, do you like it?"

Antonio tore his gaze from her and smiled at Sam.

"I'm not sure. The house is a little small, don't you think? And the wallpaper in the bathroom reminds me of Billy Bonka's chocolate factory."

Sam giggled. "If we could lick this wallpaper and it tasted like candy, then you'd have to buy it."

"Why don't you run in there and give it a taste." Antonio winked.

Frida Johnson, Antonio's realtor, sauntered in from the formal dining room with a large smile. "Isn't it lovely? First time on the market, and I know the house will go quick. Does it check all your boxes, Mr. Mendez?"

"The house is beautiful but not what I'm looking for. I'm afraid the place doesn't have enough space."

"I see plenty of square footage for a single man like yourself." Frida batted her eyelashes.

Jillian fought to keep her gag reflux in check at the over-the-top display of flirtation.

"Hopefully, I'm not a single man forever, Ms. Johnson." Antonio glanced at Jillian for a moment then away. "When Ms. Right comes along, I'd like a space big enough to make her happy." He flashed his dimples.

She rolled her eyes at his attempt at charming the realtor, but old Mrs. Johnson's face flushed as bright as the tacky pink suit she wore. Okay, so maybe Frida Johnson wasn't old, but she had a good twenty years on Antonio.

"Do you have anything else to show me this week? I'd like to find something as soon as possible." Antonio took a step toward the front door.

"How about we get together this evening for coffee, or even dinner, to talk about all of your options?"

Frida's squinted gaze flicked to Jillian for a second, before focusing once more on Antonio.

Amused annoyance swelled in her chest but not jealousy. Was her lack of jealousy because she didn't see a middle-aged woman desperate for attention as a threat, or because she didn't care? Sam's head bounced from one face to another like a dog's hungry gaze following a piece of meat. The adult innuendos bounced off his brain and left his nose wrinkled and lips pursed.

"Thanks for the invite, but I have to work early in the morning. Those planes won't fly themselves. How about another time?" Antonio chuckled and turned toward the front door.

"Wait, I thought you were taking me to dinner while Mom works." Sam narrowed his eyes and scrunched his nose.

Frida pinched her face together and glanced at Antonio through squinty eyes.

Antonio grabbed Sam and placed him in front of him like a shield. He laughed and tousled Sam's hair. "Just grabbing a quick bite, bud."

"Okay. Call and let me know when's a good time to look at more houses." Frieda gave a stiff nod, and then disappeared into the dining room and turned off the lights.

Jillian clamped her lips together to keep laughter from spilling out. With the high ceilings and tiled floors of the house, any noise she made would reach Frida's ears in no time.

Antonio opened the front door and all but pushed Sam outside.

Sam and Antonio strolled in front of her down the

tree-lined street, and snippets of conversation spiraled behind them in the subtle summer breeze. Words hit her ears every now and then, but her mind was too centered on what happened with Antonio moments before. Her emotions bounced between confusion and desire and not being even a little bit jealous of another woman's attention plastered on Antonio.

"Mom!"

Jillian blinked her brain back into focus. The short distance from the house for sale around the block to her home passed in a blur. She had no recollection of passing the familiar houses and ending in her own driveway. "I'm sorry, buddy. What did you say?"

"Do you want to eat with us? We might go to Defiance. I want a burger."

Sam widened his eyes as if a fast food burger joint was the mecca of all restaurants. She chuckled at his enthusiasm. "As tempting as greasy fast food sounds, I think I'll pass."

"Are you sure?" Antonio put his hands in the front pocket of his cargo shorts and pulled out his car keys.

Sam always got a thrill out of driving in his luxury sports car. Well, so did she. But she still wouldn't go with them tonight. "I'm heading to the store for a little bit. I was out most of the week getting everything ready for school. I want to sneak a peek at the new store. Gus doesn't like me poking around when they're working."

More like she'd wanted to avoid Jonah. He'd drained all the excitement over the store. But at this hour on a Friday evening, the construction crew would be long gone, and she could take her time reveling in all the changes.

Antonio tucked in his lips and nodded. "It's just

you and me, bud."

"Can we see a movie, too?" Sam wiggled his eyebrows.

She covered her chuckle with a cough. Sam displayed his most innocent grin for Antonio—the one he used when he was up to something.

"Sure, as long as it's okay with your mom." Antonio's gaze met hers. "Maybe a movie will convince her to join us."

Every pleading glance, every touch, every invitation—no matter how innocent—added another weight to her chest. She needed time, and she needed space. "You boys enjoy your dinner and movie, and I'll see you later. I really need to get some stuff done. School starts Monday, so the next few weeks will be crazy."

Sam jumped into Antonio's car without so much as a goodbye wave.

Antonio dipped his head and climbed into the driver's seat.

Another weight crowded into the space between her heart and lungs. She watched the red taillights down the street and then turned in the opposite direction toward the store. Kiddy Korner would still be open for another hour, but her manager would handle closing. Phyllis was like the grandmother she'd never had. She was warm, caring, and a to-the-point pain in her butt Jillian wouldn't change for the world. Jillian loved her and dreaded the day she'd retire more than Sam's high school graduation.

Twilight approached, and the streetlights flickered on around the town square. Cars drove by at a snail's pace, and the drivers searched for parking among the limited spots outside the town's only two places to eat. Jillian waved at friends, or friends of friends, who walked past but didn't stop to chitchat. Her store called with the lure of a siren's song. Before opening the door, she peeked through the front window.

A few customers loitered in the aisles, and a group of children played with the building blocks she always kept well-stocked. Pride wedged itself into a small space in her chest where guilt and pressure hadn't taken up residence. Kiddy Korner was her baby, and her baby had grown into one of the most successful businesses in Smithview.

A bell rang above the door, announcing her arrival, and she ducked her head and made a beeline for the stairs. She'd talk to Phyllis on her way out. Now, she wanted to see the birthplace of her new baby.

Darkness loomed in the narrow stairwell. No natural light slipped in from Kiddy Korner, and no light bulbs hung from the low ceiling. Wood paneling circa the 1970s covered the walls, which didn't help with the cave-like atmosphere. The old steps creaked under her weight, and she took them two at a time to reach the top. On the second floor the space opened and all claustrophobia faded. Jillian sucked in a sharp breath and wandered into the middle of the room.

Dusty plywood covered the floor, and white mud covered the newly hung drywall. The old laminate countertop and original maple cabinets took up the far wall of the kitchen. The once closed-in kitchen was now wide open, broadening the length of the room. The remaining walls corralled the small bathroom. She let her gaze linger around the space and imagined where the bookshelves would go and what color the new walls would be. Goose bumps erupted on her skin. Her new store would work.

Jillian strolled toward the fireplace. The same stone fireplace sat downstairs in Kiddy Korner, but she detoured customers from the beautifully restored stone so children wouldn't fall and crack open their heads. Here, she would highlight the feature by inviting customers to sit and read in front of a cozy fire.

Something black and square lay on the ground and caught her attention. She took three steps toward it, the subfloor bending under her weight, and crouched to pick it up. The smooth leather slid over her skin, and she flipped open the wallet to check for a driver's license. One of the workers must have dropped it.

She groaned, and the sound echoed around the empty space. "Of course, Jonah Sheffield."

Indecision bounced around her like a ping pong ball. She could leave the wallet on the ground and pretend she'd never found it, but then Jonah wouldn't get it back until Monday. As much as she didn't want to see him, she couldn't be cruel. He'd rented the old Smith house south of town. Dropping off the wallet wouldn't take her much time. Maybe she'd be lucky and he wouldn't be home. She could place the wallet in the mailbox and leave without him ever knowing she was there.

Wishful thinking made her laugh. Luck had never been on her side when dealing with Jonah Sheffield.

Chapter Seven

Boom!

The shot rang as clear as day, and its sound pierced the night sky. Jonah crouched toward the ground. He darted his gaze around his living room.

Boom!

The rigid soldier melted from his body. He sagged to the floor in front of the sofa and crushed both hands over his ears. He squeezed his eyes tight, and fast, ragged breaths shook his body.

Boom!

Images of Iraq invaded his mind. His fellow soldiers fell to the ground to escape the flying bullets, and dust flew around him. The metallic scent of blood tickled his nostrils. The crimson liquid sprayed from the limbs of those unlucky enough to avoid impending death.

The screams of his friends and brothers as they lay around him, begging for death to come as quickly as possible, surrounded him. His screams joined theirs. He screamed for his brothers to fight for their lives, he screamed for the bullets to stop, and when his screams no longer tore through him, he hung his head and wept.

Crash!

The front door burst open.

He scrambled for the gun at his hip, but nothing was there. Fear lodged in his throat. The shooter found him. His muscles tensed as he waited for death.

Gentle hands gripped his, and a soothing voice pulled at him.

Jillian.

Her gaze bore into him.

The rapid beating of his heart slowed. His breaths regulated. He concentrated on the golden flecks he always loved in her green eyes until the horrifying scene in his mind faded.

"I heard gunshots." He hated the slight tremble in his voice.

"Were they close to the house or deeper into the woods?" Jillian asked.

Her concern soothed him like salve on a burn. "The first one was farther away. The second two were closer to the house."

"I'm sure kids are in the woods hunting."

"In the middle of August? Nothing's in season." He lowered his hands from his ears and braced them on the floor.

"Around here, squirrels and rabbits are always in season. Some high school kids were probably getting in target practice before they can go after deer in a couple of months." She glanced out the window, and then back to him. "Do you want me to look around outside?"

"No, you're right." He pinched the bridge of his nose and shook his head. He took a deep breath and drew his feet close to stand.

She placed a hand on his forearm to ease him back to the floor.

"I'm fine, Jillian. Really."

"I know. But there's no rush to get up. Let's sit for a few more seconds."

"Damn it, Jillian, I said I'm fine." He jerked away, got to his feet, and paced across the cramped living room. "I hate feeling helpless and panicked about a couple of gunshots. I served as a soldier for twelve years and have been in situations I wouldn't wish on my worst enemy. I've been trained to react a certain way. Instead, I'm quivering on the floor like a child."

She rose to her feet and crossed her arms in front of her. "You have nothing to be embarrassed about, Jonah."

Frustration knotted his muscles. "You don't understand, unless you've been through what I've been through and have seen what I've seen." His footsteps pounded the floor, and he shoved his hands through his hair.

Her gaze followed him. She dropped her hands to her sides and relaxed her stance. "We've all been through tough times, Jonah. But you're right. I'll never understand your pain unless you explain it."

He stopped pacing and locked his gaze with hers. "You want me to tell you what happened in Iraq?" Anxiety pitched in his stomach. He'd never spoken about Iraq.

She shrugged, and her gaze never wavered. "Talking about what happened can't hurt. Holding everything in obviously isn't helping." She sat on the couch and patted the empty cushion bedside her.

He took one step toward her, then stopped. He'd never said the words aloud. Speaking about what happened wouldn't change anything. Opening up could even make the nightmares worse. But she was right, what he was doing wasn't helping either. Talking to Jillian could be the chance he needed to get closer and break down some of the walls she'd built. He dragged his feet the rest of the way to the couch and let out a deep sigh as he settled in beside her and placed both hands in his lap. "I've never told anyone what happened. I'm not sure I can."

Jillian placed a hand on his.

The warmth of her touch coursed through him, and he faced her. Her full lips tugged down in a slight frown and the small wrinkles at the corners of her eyes relaxed.

"Tell me as much as you want. I'm a good listener. I promise."

He leaned his head on the back of the couch. Images flooded over him, each one like a blow to his gut. He kept his gaze fixed on the ceiling. "I was on patrol one day. Me and three of my guys in one tank, and four other guys patrolling in another one. The tank I drove led the way. We made our way down a deserted road in an abandoned town. I thought I saw movement out of the corner of my eye, but I kept going."

He clenched his hands into fists and bit the inside of his mouth. Tears burned his eyes. "Then the blasts erupted. They were so close—closer than they'd ever been. When I glanced behind us, fire and smoke clouded my view."

Jillian's sharp intake of breath cut into the silence of the house.

He leaned forward and dropped his head in his hands. His mind travelled back in time while he relived the worst day of his life, and his voice trembled. "Our tank was hit next. The blast knocked us over. I tried to get out, but the door was stuck. I could hear my guys fighting back. They wanted revenge. I heard shooting, so much shooting, and I was helpless to do anything."

He stopped talking and rubbed his temples, slowing his ragged breaths. "I thought hearing the gunshots and the screaming was the worst thing I'd ever hear. But the screams were better than the silence." Saliva filled his mouth, and he swallowed hard. "When silence came, my guys, the guys I was responsible for, were dead. For hours, I was forced to lie in what I thought would be my coffin. I thought the enemy would take me and torture me for their sick pleasure before they killed me." His voice caught on a sob, and guilt twisted in his stomach.

Jillian's hand tightened on his thigh.

"I thought about my mom being told I was gone." He lifted his head and stared into Jillian's green eyes. "She'd already buried a husband. How was she supposed to bury her only son? I thought about the mothers and wives of the men who died. I was supposed to keep them alive. I was supposed to protect them."

A moment of silence passed. He wiped the tears from his face and took a steadying breath. "Moving on with your life when you're the reason someone else no longer has one to live is hard."

"You think you're the reason they aren't here?"

Her low, soft voice tightened his chest. "Yes." Jonah choked out the single word. "In my head, I know I did everything I could to save them. But my heart feels like I should have done more."

"Sometimes," Jillian said, "our hearts take longer to catch up to our minds. We have to keep moving along until it happens."

A strangled laugh spilled from his throat. "Doesn't

the mind take more time to convince?"

"Not always." Her lips hitched up in a half-smile. "Sometimes, our mind knows exactly what it needs, but the heart refuses to see it."

"My heart has always known what it wants." He shook his head and lifted his chin. Sadness weighed down his heart. "You floated into my mind a lot. Your eyes kept me calm. I concentrated on the golden specks. Focusing on the soft glow of your skin, and the longing to run my fingers through your hair kept me sane." He cupped her cheek with his hands.

Her tears trickled down his skin, and she closed her hand on his. She shut her eyes, and a soft sigh escaped her lips before she opened them again.

"You saved my life. If not for you, I don't know what would have happened. I would have gone crazy in that damn tank. But your image calmed me and made me believe I'd be okay. I had to come back here and see you again. Even after all these years, you're still the only person who can bring me peace."

His eyes burned with unshed tears. He tightened his jaw to keep them from falling again. Jillian needed to see a strong man who could face his demons, not a man who kept falling apart. He waited for her reaction, and his heart threatened to beat out of his throat.

She swallowed hard, and her lips parted.

How many times had he imagined his lips on hers? Now here she was—so close and so tempting. His blood warmed as a memory of her sweet taste flooded his senses. No matter what their future held, he needed at least one more moment where the world was right and she was his again. He leaned forward and gently pressed his lips to hers.

She tensed, and then relaxed into him as a moan purred in her throat.

The salty tears on her mouth mingled against his lips, and his heart hammered in his chest. He needed her to finally put his past behind him and move on with his life. Fisting her hair in his hands, he lowered his forehead to hers and closed his eyes. He inhaled her scent, an intoxicating mixture of vanilla and lavender. For once, the darkness didn't crash in around him.

With his eyes still closed, he leaned forward until his lips met hers once more. "Jilly," he whispered. He brushed away a strand of hair that fell across her face. His body hummed with excitement, and he trailed his hands down to her arms and lifted his mouth. Mist gathered in his eyes and clouded his vision. He gathered her into his arms, buried his face in her hair, and wept. His soul ached, but the weight he'd carried on his shoulders lifted as he pulled away. "I'm sorry. I didn't think I'd get so worked up."

Jillian wiped away her tears with the backs of her hands.

Red splotches splattered across her cheeks, and her hair stuck out wildly around her face. She'd never looked more beautiful.

She straightened but rested a hand on his knee. "You have nothing to apologize for. I'm glad I was here to listen when you needed me. You've carried a heavy burden. But, Jonah, nothing you could have done would have saved them. What happened wasn't your fault."

He flinched. "How can I believe I'm not to blame? I'm the only one who walked away. I should have saved them." Raw grief ebbed through him.

"These wounds are fresh, and you need time to

heal. Healing will happen, but it just might take a while. You already said your heart knows what it wants. Healing can't be too far behind." Jillian leaned forward, her gaze steady, and dipped her smooth brow.

He laced his fingers with hers and traced lazy circles on the back of her hand with his thumb. Her hand fit in his like a missing puzzle piece and brought the same comfort to his wounded soul now as it had when they were younger. Her small shoulder shook on a shiver against his. He smothered a chuckle. His simple touch still affected her after all these years. "What about you, Jillian? Does your heart know what it wants?"

She tucked her bottom lip behind her teeth and looked away. "I don't know if I have a good answer."

He settled her hand into his lap. "After everything I told you, you can't answer one question? Please, Jilly."

She faced him again and drew in a shaky breath. "Jonah, we have so much baggage. So much we never talked about. Things just kind of...ended. You never even—"

His stomach knotted. Jonah held up a hand. "Doesn't matter what happened back then. We were kids. Life's too short to dwell on the past. We both made mistakes. I'm willing to keep those mistakes in the past, if you are." Indecision clouded her wide green eyes.

Jillian reared back her head and squinted. "Our mistakes weren't small, even if we were young. They shaped my entire life. I don't know if I can forget them."

"I wouldn't want you to forget them, but why rehash things we can't change? I want you in my life,

Jilly—baggage and all." He squeezed her hand and his blood pumped furiously through his veins. Talking to Jillian about their future was why he'd come home, and his entire life depended on her answer. "I don't want the sins of our past to keep us from having a future together."

She dropped her gaze. "I'm not sure what kind of future I can give you. Things are a little complicated in my life right now."

Her palm grew moist in his hand. No complication in this world would keep him away. "What do you mean?"

"My ex-husband is moving back to town, and he'd like to give us another chance."

His heart dropped to his stomach. Dylan and Meg warned him. He couldn't get in her way if she wanted to put her family back together. He pulled away his hand and wiped the sweat on his thighs. "Do you want to get back together with him?"

She shrugged. "I don't know what I want. This"— she waved a hand between them—"is completely unexpected. Antonio returning is just as unexpected. I need some time to wrap my mind around having you both back in town."

He couldn't help but smile at the irony. "Once you make up your mind about what you want, will you have to convince your heart? Or does your heart already know?"

Blush colored her cheeks, and she glanced through thick lashes. "I can't say what you want to hear right now."

"I want to know how you feel," he whispered. She might not give him the answer he wanted, but she could give him a small kernel of hope. If she still felt something for him, no matter how small or confusing, he'd wait as long as he had to for the rest to fall into place. They were meant to be together.

She sucked in a breath. "Honestly, something's happening between us I don't understand. My feelings scare me. But I have other things to figure out first before I jump into anything." She twisted her mouth into a grimace and shook her head. "I don't just have myself to think about."

Her voice was wispy as air and sent a chill down his spine. "I understand, but just so you know, I don't need to figure out anything. You've always been the one for me."

She lifted her brows, and her lips curved into a smirk. "You've always been a smooth talker." She rested her head on his shoulder and placed a hand on his leg.

Desire pooled in his stomach, and he swallowed it. He'd give her the time she needed. Leaning down, he placed a kiss in her hair before resting his chin on the top of her head. He closed his eyes, and for the first time in as long as he could remember, he wasn't afraid.

Chapter Eight

Bzzz-bzzz-bzzz.

Jillian fluttered her eyelids and urged the sleepy muscles in her arms to smash her alarm clock against the floor. She flung off the covers and reached for her phone on the nightstand so she could shut off the alarm she'd set the night before. Refusing to open her eyes against the morning sun's glare, she ran clumsy fingers over the random bric-a-brac beside her bed before she finally found her phone and hit snooze.

To hide from the day a bit longer, Jillian buried her head under the comforter and glued her eyes shut. No one should get up this early on their day off, but the blaring alarm clock she'd set the night before didn't care. She opened her eyes, threw back the covers, and shut off her alarm. Damn Catie for making her wake up at such an ungodly hour to jog. Summer was almost over, so what did it matter if she had a few extra pounds hanging around to keep her company over the winter?

Reality crashed on her in the form of a white down blanket. She had two very handsome men vying for her attention. Even if she didn't have a clue how to handle the situation, looking her best while figuring it out wouldn't be a bad idea. Before she could talk herself out of exercising Jillian jumped out of bed, threw on her workout clothes, and hurried to her front porch to wait for Catie.

Even this early in the morning, warmth hugged her body and welcomed her outside. The sun barely shimmered above the horizon, casting shades of pink and orange against the sky to beat back the night for another full day. The sky might be beautiful, but the scenery didn't make her like the morning any better.

She set her water bottle on the floor beside the swing and cradled a cup of coffee in her hands. Steam wafted up her nostrils. She inhaled deeply and let the smell wake up her brain cells before the caffeine hit her palette.

"Good morning, sunshine." Catie bounded up the porch stairs in one leap and not one piece of auburn hair fell out of place.

Catie's cheerful voice matched the high-pitched chirping of the birds catching the proverbial worm. If Jillian didn't love her so much, she'd smack the too-wide smile off her beautiful face.

Jillian grunted and lifted her favorite oversized mug to her mouth. The hot liquid coated her tongue and slid down her throat. The punch of the strong, black coffee would provide the pep in her step she'd need to get through her jog. When she returned, she'd reward herself with another cup with her favorite creamer. The thought gave her something to look forward to.

Catie chuckled and joined her on the swing. "Aren't you pleasant this morning?"

Jillian glanced from the corner of her eyes at her friend.

Catie's curls bounced on the top of her head, and she used her feet to push the swing back and forth.

Coffee spilled from the top of Jillian's mug and sloshed onto her yoga plants. "I'll be in an even worse mood if you keep making me spill my coffee." Sleep made her words come out slow, and she planted her heels on the floorboards to stop the swing.

"I'll never understand why people don't like mornings. Mornings are so full of possibilities." Catie drew in a deep breath and lifted her gaze toward the sky.

"The morning will still be here in a few hours and will hold all the possibilities you want." Jillian slurped more coffee and prayed it kicked in soon. She usually needed at least half a cup to wake her up.

"Is Sam still sleeping?" Catie pushed her feet against the wooden planks and moved back the swing.

Jillian squeezed her leg to make her stop.

"Sorry. It's some sort of natural reaction to sitting on this thing."

"Not for me. And yes, Sam's asleep. I told him last night I'd be out of the house for a little bit this morning. I locked the door, and I have no doubt the brat will be sound asleep when we get back."

A soft vibration hummed against her hip. She pulled the phone from the waistband of her pants and glanced at a picture of Antonio above his contact information. Panic gripped her heart. Antonio never called her this early unless something was wrong. She thrust her coffee mug toward Catie and pressed the answer button. "Hello? Are you okay?"

"I'm fine. Did I wake you?"

Antonio's husky voice calmed her nerves and made her mad at the same time. Adrenaline seeped from her pores, but her heart beat a little too quickly. She leaned her head back on the hard wood of the swing. "No, I'm awake. What's going on?"

Catie jutted her chin forward and held up her free hand in a who's-on-the-phone gesture.

Jillian covered the speaker on her phone and mouthed, "Antonio." Catie's hazel eyes narrowed.

"I didn't mean to scare you, but I got a call from Frida. A house came on the market late last night I'm dying to see. I got someone to cover my flight this morning and wondered if you and Sam could see it with me?"

Antonio's voice rose an octave with each word he spoke. The inflection conveyed how much he wanted them with him. Jillian scratched the soft material covering her thigh with a short, stubby fingernail. Looking at houses last night with Antonio had been fun, but he needed to make this decision without her. Anxiety swelled in her stomach like a balloon inflating. He couldn't depend on her to pick a house because their future was unclear. The more he asked of her, the more he pushed her away. "I don't think we can make it this morning. Catie and I have plans. She's here already, actually." Catie's perfectly tweezed eyebrows rose to her forehead.

Jillian waved off her scrutiny and returned her focus to her thigh.

"Okay."

How he infused one word with so much disappointment was beyond her, and a jab of guilt sucker punched her gut.

"What about afterward? I'm dying to see the new space, and then we can get lunch."

Jillian sucked in a deep breath. He wouldn't give up, and she didn't want to be mean. "Okay. Sam and I will meet you at Kiddy Korner at noon." She hung up the phone and lifted her gaze to Catie. The heat of Catie's questioning gaze burned a hole in the side of her face.

"You planning on jogging all morning with me?"

"Sorry, you were a convenient excuse. Antonio wanted Sam and me to see a house with him, and I don't think it's a good idea." Grabbing back her coffee mug, Jillian concentrated on the warmth seeping into her skin and not the now-familiar confusion swimming in her mind.

"We're finally talking about this?" Catie steepled her fingers and tapped them together in her best Dr. Evil impression. "Good, I'm dying to find out what's going on. And once we're done talking about Antonio, you can spill the beans on Jonah."

Jillian's body tensed. "What about Jonah?"

"Don't play dumb." Catie dropped her hands to her sides and narrowed her eyes. "Everyone in town's been talking about how he hit Blake last week, and you jumped in and saved him. I want the dirty details."

Despite the memories of her recent talks with Jonah rushing back, Jillian chuckled. "Why didn't you ask me?"

Catie smirked. "Because I know you. You'll talk when you're ready. If I tried too soon, you would have shot me down quicker than a high school cheerleader shutting down the chess club captain."

Jillian shook her head. "I'm still not ready to talk about Jonah, but I don't think I have a choice. Besides, I don't know what I want to do about everything that's been dumped in my lap."

"Start with Antonio. Why would you want to see this house with him?"

Catie softened her tone, and Jillian almost whimpered with relief. She'd held in everything for days, and she didn't realize until now how much she needed to let it out. "Antonio is moving back to town to be near Sam, and he wants to reconcile." The words flew out on a rush of emotion—quick and jumbled together.

Catie whistled and widened her eyes. "Do you want to be with him?"

"I don't know." Jillian lifted her shoulders. "Being a family again would be nice. Sam would love having his dad with him all the time."

"But do you love him?" Catie grabbed her hand and squeezed.

The quietness of the morning collided against the voices in her head. She tried to separate everything and focus on the rustling leaves and the singing birds, but the morning noises didn't help. She searched for the answer to Catie's question but couldn't find it.

"I think you have the answer."

"How can I really know for sure if I love him or not?" Jillian sighed.

"That's bull, and you know it. Either you love someone, or you don't." Catie shrugged.

"But maybe I could love him," Jillian whispered, the words ringing hollow and untrue. As much as she'd wanted to love Antonio one time in her life, her heart had always belonged to Jonah. Whether she wanted it to or not. "I need time to figure out what I want. He's such a good friend, and I haven't considered the possibility of more in a very long time. We've always been on good terms, and moving back to Smithview solves the biggest problem in our marriage. He'll actually be around."

"Honey, do you really think Antonio's work schedule was the biggest problem with your marriage?" Catie tilted her head to the side and lifted her lips in a half-smile.

Jillian squeezed her eyes to block out the pain Catie's words caused, but closing her eyes couldn't keep the truth of Catie's statement from slamming into her heart. She opened them again and glanced at Catie. "No, but we could work on the other problems that tore us apart."

"Even if the problem now also lives in Smithview?" Catie dipped her chin and pursed her lips.

Jillian stood and paced back and forth across the porch. The floorboards squeaked, and she cursed the fact that the porch wasn't bigger. All of Catie's questions caused energy to spark to life inside and left her body jittery. "Jonah shouldn't have any bearing on what I decide to do about Antonio." Catie's soft laugh made her stop and turn.

Catie covered her mouth and stifled the sound. "Sorry. I couldn't help but chuckle. Jonah not having an effect on your decision is like the rain not affecting how the grass grows. What did you two talk about last week?"

Jillian drooped her shoulders and leaned against the railing. "Last week he made me mad. I acted on impulse, and he told me what he thought happened to our relationship."

"Which was?" Catie's gaze locked with hers.

"I thought he wasn't good enough for me. Can you believe him?" Hysteria caught steam, and her voice rose.

Catie bit into her lip and widened her eyes, pausing a moment before she asked, "What did happen? One day you were the most in-love, disgusting couple I'd ever seen and the next, he was gone and you were a mess."

Jillian set down her cup on the railing. She'd never told anyone what had happened with Jonah except for Antonio. Talking about their break-up was too hard. But she had to tell Catie something, even if only a tiny piece of the puzzle. "I didn't make it to Jonah's house in time to say good-bye the day he left for boot camp. Things had happened earlier in the day. Things I needed to tell him but never got the chance. Things I needed to wrap my mind around before I could write and explain. When I finally sent him a letter to explain why I hadn't shown up, he never responded." Tears collected in her throat and made it hard to breath. She bit into the tender flesh of her cheek to keep them down. She'd cried a thousand tears for the love she'd lost and didn't want to cry anymore.

Catie straightened on the swing, and the corners of her eyes crinkled. "What happened?"

Jillian shook her head. She couldn't talk about the rest. "It doesn't matter. But now Jonah is here, and he wants to put the past behind us and start fresh. I don't know if I can." She lifted fingers to her lips, and her toes curled. He'd kissed her last night. A simple kiss between old lovers that had left her breathless. His lips on hers awakened a desire so strong she'd spent the entire night wrapped in a fantasy that died twelve years ago. Her heart constricted as if a boa wrapped around it. She sniffed back all the tears and the memories and the emotion Jonah's kiss evoked. Tears and memories and emotion Antonio had never come close to bringing out.

"Are you still in love with Jonah?"

Her heart stopped beating for a moment. Not because she didn't know the answer, but because she was afraid to admit the answer to herself. She tapped the toe of her tennis shoe against the floor, and she focused her gaze on the motion. "I've never stopped loving him, but loving him doesn't mean he's the one I should be with. He destroyed me, Catie."

"I know." Catie leaned against the rail beside her. "I was there. But do you think explaining things would help? Even if he doesn't need to hear what you have to say, sharing your truth could give you closure to move forward with Jonah or move on with Antonio."

Jillian shrugged. Jonah had enough on his mind right now, and he'd made it clear as crystal he didn't want to dredge up their past. Dumping the baggage on him that weighed her down for so long wouldn't make her feel any better, and it would only drag him further down a miserable path he was desperate to get off. "Sometimes, closure isn't an option." She glanced down at her coffee cup. The liquid speed was almost gone, and yet fatigue lingered in every ounce of her body. "Do we still have to go on a stupid jog?"

Catie wrapped an arm around her shoulders and pulled her close. "Did you make up all this so I'd feel sorry for you and let you go back to sleep?"

Jillian threw back her head, and her deep, belly-aching laugh bounced off the covered porch and lifted her spirits. "You caught me."

"I knew it." Catie dropped her arm and bounced her shoulder off Jillian's. "You'll figure out everything. Give yourself some time."

Jillian nodded but didn't respond. The words she'd said to Jonah the night before floated back. Maybe she needed to take her own advice and give her mind a little time to catch up to her heart. The only problem was her heart had led her down a path of destruction before, so how could she trust it again?

She glanced down at her watch. Four hours until she had to meet Antonio at Kiddy Korner. Maybe the time had come to stop listening to her heart and do what made more sense—time to put her broken family back together. But even as the idea entered her mind, she couldn't deny how her lips tingled with the memory of Jonah's kiss. She'd never imagined Jonah's lips would be on hers again, and now that they had, could she go the rest of her life without them?

Chapter Nine

—I'll be there in ten minutes. Order me a beer—

Jonah threw his phone on the passenger seat of his truck, climbed inside, and drove toward town. Sweat clung to his brow, and he blasted the air conditioner. After all his years in Iraq, he was more used to the dry heat of the desert. The Ohio air in August was suffocating. He rolled down his window, and the breeze smacked him in the face and cooled him off, even as the cold air from the vents pushed the heat from the rest of his truck.

On his way into town, he passed Coop's Dairy Farm. The mooing of cattle carried into his truck, and he tugged his lips into a smile. He'd forgotten so much about his hometown. Passing the farm brought an onslaught of memories. The scent of manure and hay stung his nostrils, and he coughed to expel the mixture from his nose. His smile quickly morphed into a scowl, and he rolled up his window. Next time, he'd keep up the windows until he got into town.

At the town square, he pulled his truck into a parking spot and climbed out. He cast a quick glance over his shoulder.

Celeste, the owner of the floral store and his mom's best friend, bustled in the display window.

He waved, turned the corner, and his feet transformed to lead.

Jillian stepped out of Kiddy Korner with her hand on her son's shoulder. Her white summer dress caught the breeze, revealing slim legs. A tall, dark-haired man appeared behind them, and his hand lingered against the small of Jillian's back. Sam ran ahead, and Jillian laughed up at the man as he matched her stride. His hand left her back but stayed annoyingly close to her side.

Antonio.

Irritation pulsed through Jonah, and jealousy burrowed in his gut. He gnawed at the inside of his cheek, and he dug his thumbnails into his palm. The urge to grab Antonio by the back of his neck and yank him away from Jillian hummed through his body. He took a deep breath and counted to ten. Once the three were safely inside That's Amore, he'd calmed enough to continue on his way to the bar. He shook his head and tried his hardest to get the image of Jillian's happy smile out of his mind. Together, the three were a family. His conscience nagged.

The bell above the door of The Village Idiot dinged, and he stepped inside.

Dylan waved from the bar.

Jonah took a seat, picked up the waiting beer and lifted the mug to his lips. The cool liquid flowed down his throat and the bitterness coated his mouth and warmed his blood. He set down the mug and wiped the residual moisture off his lip with the back of his hand.

"Damn, you just downed half of your beer. You okay?" Dylan cradled his mug in his hands and leaned his forearms on the bar.

"Yeah, I'm fine."

Dylan pulled together his brows.

"What?" Jonah snapped. He rubbed at the tension building in his forehead. "I saw Jillian with her ex-husband. They looked a little too cozy."

"Huh."

"Huh? That's all you have to say?"

"Meg and I told you he was moving back to town. You can't be too surprised to see them together."

Jonah dropped his hands to the mug and mimicked Dylan's body language. "He's not wasting any time claiming her. His hands were all over her. She told me last night she needed time to figure out what she wanted to do."

"I didn't know you and Jillian spent time together." Dylan tilted his head to the side and the corners of his eyes crinkled.

"We didn't plan to see each other. She showed up at my place, and one thing led to another."

Dylan held his beer half way to his mouth and froze. "I need a little more information. What do you mean one thing led to another?"

Jonah's body stiffened, and he slapped Dylan on the back of the head. "Get your mind out of the gutter." He cleared his throat and shifted on his stool. "I was having a panic attack when she got there, and I ended up telling her about what happened in Iraq."

Dylan choked on his beer, and rivulets of amber liquid spilled onto the bar. "You've never even told me what happened. How'd it go?"

Emotion clawed at his throat, and he stared into his beer. "Good, I guess. I wasn't expecting to tell her anything, but the story kind of spilled out. I hate to admit it, but a weight lifted from my chest. I mean, don't get me wrong, I still feel horrible—just a little less so."

Dylan laughed and patted him on the back. "Your problems will never get better if you don't learn to deal with them. But I'm confused. How did talking about Iraq lead to Jillian talking about Antonio?"

Jonah snaked a hand around to the back of his neck, and he groaned. He hadn't told anyone the real reason he'd come home. Not even Dylan. "Well, I was pretty emotional after talking about everything, and things were brought up. One of those things being how I feel about Jillian."

"Dude." Dylan narrowed his eyes.

Jonah bristled at Dylan's low tone. "What am I supposed to do? Act like I'm not still in love with her? What's the point of pretending? I've been miserable for a long time, and if she's the person who can make me happy, why shouldn't I tell her?"

Dylan lifted his shoulders and smoothed the lines of his face. "Maybe because you two broke up a long time ago, and the aftermath wasn't pretty. Did you talk about what happened between you two? She broke your heart, man."

Jonah ran his tongue over his top teeth and took a deep breath. "What happened between us back then doesn't matter. Like you said, it was a long time ago. We were so young, and we both made mistakes. We have no reason to relive it."

"If that's the way you want it. What did Jillian say when you told her how you felt?"

"She said things are complicated. She told me about Antonio, and she has more than herself to think about. I respect her situation, I really do, but seeing them together...man, I don't know." He lifted his gaze and met Dylan's intense stare. "What if I end up being the reason her kid doesn't have his parents together?"

Dylan rested a hand on Jonah's shoulder and squeezed. "Jillian not being with Antonio would never be on you. You're not the reason Jillian and her husband got a divorce, and Jillian needs to decide who she wants to be with. If she chooses Antonio, you'll have to deal with it. If she chooses you, then Sam will be lucky to have two guys in his life who love the hell out of him."

Jonah snorted. Dylan's logic might make sense, but it wouldn't to a kid who wanted his parents back together. Hopefully, Jillian would give him another chance then he could work on winning over her son. "I don't even know him yet."

"No, but if you and Jillian get back together, you will. Trust me, he's a good kid. Everyone in town is in love with him. It won't be long before you are, too."

His heart clenched, and he took another drink. "I hope you're right." Doubt tightened his gut. He hadn't been around kids since he'd been one. Winning over one couldn't be as easy as Dylan made it sound—no matter how lovable Sam was. If Sam didn't want Jonah around, Jillian probably wouldn't him around either.

****

The days passed slowly, each one leaving Jonah with not enough time spent with Jillian. Every day he poured his blood, sweat, and anxiety into his work. Gus was right. Using physical labor as a release helped to keep his mind focused and his nerves in check. Instead of the sharp rap of a hammer making his body jerk with apprehension, he'd count the number of times the hammer hit whatever the hell it pounded. If tension wound its way around his neck like a noose, he'd find something to hit or cut or create until the noose loosened.

With Jillian's son busy at school, the time she spent coming upstairs to check on the progress dwindled. Jonah bounced between wanting to find her and talk about her day and wanting to give her the space she'd asked for. The problem was, he had no clue how much time she spent with Antonio.

A couple of weeks passed, and he found himself sick and tired of twiddling his thumbs. A coy smile or a pretty blush to her cheeks when he waved wasn't enough anymore. He needed to spend real time with her and find out what was going on in her head. A deep growl sounded in his stomach and reminded him he hadn't eaten all day. He glanced at his watch. Lunch time. An idea blossomed, and he hurried down the stairs and prayed Jillian would be in her office.

Stepping through her open office door, he leaned against the doorframe and crossed his arms over his chest to hide his trembling hands. She made him more nervous now than she had when they were younger.

Her gaze never left the computer screen in front of her and her fingers flew over the keys, the soft tinkering sound filled the room.

"Hey, Jilly." His voice boomed among the four walls.

Jillian snapped up her head. A long strand of hair fell across her forehead and in front of her widened eyes.

To keep from brushing her hair to the side, he curled his fingers into his palms.

Her pink tongue swiped across her lower lip.

The muscles in his stomach contracted. He kept his pose casual even as his insides screamed to take her in his arms and kiss her.

"Hi."

The croak in her throat eased his throbbing nerves.

He nodded toward her computer to take his mind off the path it ventured down. "What are you working on?"

"Inventory. I can hardly keep the store stocked right now, and I have all the new stuff to order for upstairs." She pushed stray hair off her face, and then rested her fingers beneath her chin, propping up her head.

"Are you normally busy this time of year? Or are people being nosy and stealing a glimpse of the store?"

"We're usually busy once school starts. I always keep the reading list for all of the local schools in stock." She lifted her head from her hands and picked up a purple plastic pouch from her desk. "Not to mention all the novelty items pre-teen girls have to have. Do you know how much I can charge for a pencil case?"

He chuckled and stepped away from the doorframe to grab the glittery pencil case from her hands. He studied the frilly plastic. "I have no idea. Can't say I've ever had much need for one of these things. You can only fit like two pencils in here."

"All the more reason to buy two."

Jillian's grin spread as wide as the Cheshire cat. Shaking his head, Jonah clucked his mock disapproval. "You should be ashamed of yourself. Overcharging young girls and stealing their babysitting money." He threw the pencil case on the desk and took a seat in the only chair across from her.

Jillian lifted her hands, and her wide grin stayed plastered on her face. "Capitalism is a wonderful thing."

A soft knock caught both of their attention.

Jonah twisted in his seat and found the kind gray eyes of the manager of Kiddy Korner. Phyllis would look more at home with a gingham apron around her ample waist and a freshly baked apple pie in her hands than working in a bookstore.

Her gaze landed on him briefly before she softened her facial features and met Jillian's raised brows. "I'm back from lunch. We'll be slow for a while if you want to grab a bite to eat." She rapped on the doorframe twice with a closed fist and then disappeared into the store.

Jonah could have kissed Phyllis's rosy cheeks in gratitude for the perfect opening. He'd wanted to ask Jillian to lunch but had lost his nerve as soon as he'd reached her office. He'd be a fool not to seize the opportunity. He shifted in his seat, and the slim legs of the chair scraped against the floor. Sweat tickled his palms, and he wiped them on his thighs, and then cringed at the wet marks streaking up his legs. "I was heading out to That's Amore to get some pizza. Want to come?"

Jillian bit into her stubby thumbnail and landed her gaze everywhere but on him. "I don't know."

"All I want is to talk a little. Spend some time together. Construction's almost done. It'd be nice to hear what you have in mind for the store once we're gone." He kept his tone soft and his voice low, afraid he'd spook her like a wild mare if he came on too strong.

Her gaze finally flitted toward him.

He held his breath. If she said no, he was doomed. Soon, he would be out of excuses to see or bump into her. For long enough he'd kept their encounters polite. He needed to make a move now, or who knew when he'd have the perfect combination of opportunity and iron-clad nerve.

Okay, not so iron-clad. A cold sweat gathered on the back of his neck, and he'd rather be carrying an assault rifle and staring into the eyes of his enemy than waiting for the indecision to leave Jillian's clouded eyes and tight-lipped smile. At least the enemies he left behind in Iraq made their intentions clear. With Jillian, he had no idea where he stood. His stomach growled and cut into the tense silence.

Jillian chuckled. "Now you're even getting your stomach to talk me into going out with you?"

"Trust me, no part of me wants to talk you into anything. Either you want to get a pizza with me or you don't. No pressure." He stood and stared down. Damn, she was beautiful. Jamming his hands into his pockets, he'd give her ten more seconds. Then he'd go. He didn't want to force her into anything, and he had to cling to a little bit of pride.

Jillian glanced at her computer, and she moved fingers across the keyboard. Then she stood, grabbed her purse from on top of the file cabinet, and finally met his gaze. Her brow furrowed, and her lips curved into a small smile. "All right. Let's get some pizza."

He wanted to jump into the air and click his heels together like the chimney sweep in the movie about the singing nanny, but he resisted. Instead, he swept a hand through the air and gestured toward the door. His cheeks hurt from the smile plastered on his face. "After you, Jilly."

Chapter Ten

Slipping into That's Amore with Jonah was like taking a step back in time. An invisible wall of garlic and oregano greeted them at the threshold, and saliva filled her mouth. Red-and-white tablecloths covered the tables, and a flood of memories washed over her.

Their first date had been here. Neither of them was old enough to drive yet, and both rode their bikes into town to meet for dinner. Her parents had been furious when they'd found out. She wasn't supposed to date until she was sixteen, but she didn't care. She had done anything to spend time with Jonah.

A hush fell over the busy crowd.

Even the cool air blasting from the overhead vents couldn't cool the heat radiating inside her. Maybe having lunch with Jonah at the hottest lunch spot in town hadn't been such a good idea. Everyone in Smithview would soon be talking about her lunch date with Jonah. But she couldn't let gossip bother her. She wasn't a child but a grown woman who could spend time with whomever she chose. Straightening her spine, she walked with her head high to the only free table beside the large picture window overlooking the town square and sat.

A middle-aged waitress rushed over with two plastic-covered menus.

Jonah slid into the seat across from her and waved

away the menus. "We'll take a medium pepperoni and mushroom pizza. Cooked a little extra if you don't mind." He glanced at her. "Do you want a cola?"

She nodded and tried to hide her amusement. After all these years, he still remembered her order. Tingles of excitement burst in the pit of her stomach.

He ordered a cola for them both.

"Cooked a little longer, huh? I remember someone use to give me the hardest time about having pizza cooked too long." She smirked and watched him through narrowed eyes as their drinks arrived.

"I hate to admit the fact, but after eating it burnt for so many years, I prefer it that way."

She leaned back and folded her arms across her chest. The booth crinkled against her skin with every movement. "I'm glad you finally realized I was right."

"You were right about most things, Jillian."

His intense gaze made her squirm. She brushed her hair over her shoulder and focused on placing her napkin on her lap. "Try telling my son I'm usually right. He might agree on the pizza, but he thinks I have no clue about everything else."

"How old is Sam again? You told me when I met him, but his age slipped my mind."

His soft voice had her lifting her gaze. His blue eyes sparkled, and her muscles melted against the seat. "Eight, going on twenty. We haven't hit the teenage years yet, and he's already Mr. Attitude. When I had a boy, I thought I would escape all the moodiness and attitude associated with teenage girls. I had no idea boys can be just as bad."

"I'm sure he'll snap out of it fast. He seems like a good kid. Every time I see him, he's sitting quietly and reading. I don't think you could trust most eight-year-old boys to be so well mannered."

"Thanks. Raising him alone has been a struggle. I'm always balancing between being the enforcer as well as the nurturer." She absently twirled the straw bobbing in her drink.

A smile lifted his lips, and he ran a hand through his hair.

The shaggy cut reminded her of the lean, gangly teenager he once was.

"You should talk to my mom sometime. Her circumstances were different, but she knows a thing or two about having to be both mother and father to a young boy. Lord knows I didn't make it easy."

"I think your mom would agree she was pretty lucky. She's done a great job with all three of you. Talking to her is not a bad idea, though. I'll have to the next time I see her. Although I might not need to now." His pupils darkened, and his easy grin slid into the same pursed-lipped expression Sam gave when she annoyed him.

Jonah cleared his throat and dropped his gaze to the table for a beat before meeting her gaze again. "I'm sure having Antonio back in town will help a lot."

Jillian scratched her nose to cover her grimace. Unease sloshed around her stomach with her soda. Talking to Jonah about Antonio was the last thing she wanted. "I hope so. I also hope having him around will ease a little of the pressure, and guilt, I've felt about being all Sam has."

Jonah shifted in his seat and cleared his throat. "I'm sure Sam is excited to have his father around, but you aren't all he has. He has two grandparents who I'm sure spoil him rotten. We both know how spoiled you were."

"I can't believe you called me spoiled." She pushed out her chin and lifted her nose but couldn't quite erase her smile.

"Don't act so wounded." Jonah smirked and a laugh coated his words. "You were the envy of every kid in town. You always got the best toys and coolest clothes. Lots of attention and toys are the perks of being an only child."

She lifted her straw from the glass and flicked the tip toward him. "Yeah, yeah, yeah. Being an only child also comes with no siblings to play with or whisper to about how your parents drive you crazy. I'll never have the bond with anyone like you have with Meg and Emma." She sighed and lifted a shoulder. "I was always so jealous of you and your sisters."

"Emma and Meg always thought of you as a sister. Hell, they still do. I know you guys still talk. Emma can't wait to see the store. She's coming home this weekend and has been hounding me to ask if she can get a tour of the new space."

The waitress hurried over and set the pizza in the middle of the table.

Jillian leaned forward and inhaled. Garlic and the smell of slightly burnt cheese wafted up her nose, and she pressed her lips together to keep the saliva in her mouth. She grabbed a slice and set it on her plate. "I'm so glad you brought up Emma. I hoped I could convince her to come look at the store. I need some input on design ideas. I have an idea in my head of what I want, but I'm not always the greatest at making my vision a reality. Emma's a genius with decorating."

Jonah rolled his eyes. "Please don't tell her she's a genius. Her head's already big enough."

Jillian pressed her lips together to stop laughter from spilling from her mouth. "Stop it. She deserves every bit of praise. I should text her and ask her to come by when she has a chance. How long will she be in town?"

"Four or five days. She'll have plenty of time to stop by."

Jillian picked up her pizza and glanced at him through her lashes.

He licked a smudge of marinara from the corner of his mouth.

Tingling sensations erupted in hot bursts up and down her arms, and her blood grew warm. She bit into her pizza and concentrated on the burst of garlic and oregano on her tongue. She hoped he hadn't caught the flush that crept onto her cheeks. She dared a glance across the table, and their gazes locked.

He reached for her hand.

She dropped her pizza and shot from her seat, the intensity of his touch causing too many sensations to course through her body. Her chest rose and fell with her ragged breathes, but she couldn't tear her gaze from him. Her body's reaction was natural, but she hadn't figured out what future she wanted for herself and Sam. "I think it's time to head back."

A lazy smile formed on his lips. "Whatever you want, Jilly."

His eyes clouded over with the same look he'd had when they were teenagers about to enjoy their first physical experience of love. He wasn't talking about ending their lunch. A shiver of excitement coursed through her body.

Tap-tap-tap.

Jillian tore her gaze from Jonah and glanced out the window. All the blood drained from her face and she gripped the table again, but this time to steady herself.

Antonio knocked on the window and then rocked back on his heels on the sidewalk with Blake Thomas at his side. Blake's face hung toward the ground, but he couldn't quite hide his smirk.

Antonio's dark eyes could have melted the glass between them from his laser-like gaze, and he pressed his lips together so hard they puckered like duck lips. If she wasn't so irritated by his sudden appearance, his expression would be comical.

Jonah raised an eyebrow and followed her line of vision then faced her with a hard-set jaw and narrowed gaze. "You meeting your ex?"

His clipped words cut at her like a dozen paper cuts. She shook her head. "I didn't know he was in town again."

Jonah threw his half-eaten piece of pizza on the table and wiped the marinara from his mouth with a napkin. "I've lost my appetite. I think you're right. Time to go."

"You're upset because my ex-husband randomly showed up? Seriously?" A sudden burst of anger erupted. She hadn't asked for any of this. She'd been honest about where she stood with him and Antonio. "You're acting like a wounded teenage girl? I didn't ask him to come by. I didn't plan on leaving lunch with you so I could meet him. What I do with *my* time shouldn't matter."

Jonah sucked in a deep breath and dropped his

head. "You're right. I'm sorry. You can spend time with whomever you want, and I'm happy to spend a little time with you today. I don't want to end our lunch on a bad note. I hoped—"

Tap-tap-tap.

"What?" She lifted her hands and clenched her jaw as her blood pressure spiked. She glanced again at Antonio.

Antonio took a step back, and his face fell.

Jillian sighed and focused on Jonah. "Can we talk more later? I need to see what he wants. Something might be wrong with Sam."

"Doubt that," Jonah mumbled under his breath and wadded his napkin in his fist.

She pursed her lips together in her best I'm-a-mom-don't-mess-with-me look and stared. "What did you say?"

Jonah cleared his throat, but he couldn't hide the laughter in his voice when he asked, "Can I call you later?"

She bit back a smile of her own. "Sure." She plunged a hand into her purse and retrieved a business card.

He grabbed the card and closed his hand around hers.

Her blood warmed and rushed through her veins.

"I got the check." Jonah tipped his head toward the window. "See what the hell he wants."

"Are you sure? I can pay for my share." She cocked her head to the side and studied him. Jonah was never one to back down. He was more likely to charge in going a hundred miles an hour and assess the damage later than sit quietly and let something slip through his fingers.

"Go. I'll talk to you later."

She smiled and squeezed his hand before hurrying out of the restaurant. Dread curdled in her stomach. She hadn't discussed Jonah returning to Smithview with Antonio and, until now, wasn't sure if he even was aware Jonah had come home. Hot, muggy air greeted her, but Antonio's icy demeanor had chills running down her spine.

"What the hell's going on?" Antonio blasted the words.

Two old women with their worn faces bowed together in conversation lifted their heads and stared with opened mouths.

Ignoring the gawkers, Jillian glanced inside and breathed a sigh of relief Jonah had been considerate enough to move away from the window. She nodded at Blake before taking a step closer to Antonio and lowering her voice to barely above a whisper. "Excuse me?"

"You didn't even have the decency to tell me Jonah was back in town, and now you're out with him? Seriously, Jillian, I'm uprooting my entire life for you and Sam."

"Nobody asked you to move here." She hurled the heated words from her mouth. She wouldn't allow him to throw his moving back to Smithview in her face every time he got upset.

"Umm, I'm heading out. Give me a call, Antonio. Nice to see you, Jillian." Blake ducked his head and fled in the opposite direction.

Jillian kept her gaze trained on Blake's back. "What are you doing with Blake?"

Antonio snorted. "He's the only person in this town who doesn't avoid me like the plague, and now I know why."

Uneasiness settled over her like an itchy blanket. "Be careful. He likes to cause trouble."

Antonio shook his head and snaked a hand through his hair. "You mean like helping a guy by giving him a place to crash? Sounds like a horrible person."

Jillian faced Antonio and something didn't sit right. She'd never understand what Meg saw in Blake. He'd always been a trouble maker, and Meg deserved better. "You're staying with him? I didn't even know you two were friends."

"It's clear we don't know everything about each other." Antonio lifted his chin to peer over her head and glance inside then reconnected their gazes. "How could you be interested in him after he attacked Blake? After everything he did? I was there for you when that jerk left. I picked up the pieces."

Adrenaline pumped through her and left her trembling. She had done nothing wrong, and she refused to be treated like the bad guy. Especially when her history with Antonio had its own rocky moments. "And then you left, too. But you left me with a toddler to raise all by myself while you did whatever the hell you wanted. Leaving open the door to come in whenever you chose so your son wouldn't forget your face."

Antonio reared back his head, and the red invading his face left, replaced by a pasty, white sheen. "Wow. I never knew how you really felt." He raised his fingers and rubbed the wrinkles out of his forehead.

She took a deep breath and filled her lungs with the

thick air. Her temper flared to life, and she took a minute to stomp it down to smoldering coals instead of a raging fire. "You've done your best, but doing all you can doesn't mean I've had an easy time. So, if moving back here means you'll constantly bring up all the changes you made in your life to benefit me and Sam, I don't want to hear it."

Antonio dropped his hand and took a step toward her. "I'm moving back because I love you and Sam. I want us to be a family."

"Enough." She held up her palm to stop any more words from spilling out of his mouth. "I know what you want, and I still don't know if us getting back together is a good idea."

"Because of him?" He lifted his chin toward the window.

Disgust coated his voice, and she cringed. "No, because of you. Because of me. Hell, because of Sam. The same things that make us"—Jillian waved a hand between them—"a great idea are the same things that make it a horrible idea." Her phone rang, and she groaned when she didn't recognize the number. "Give me a second. I need to see who's calling." She turned for privacy and answered the phone. "Hello?"

"Hey, Jilly. Want to get dinner with me Saturday night?"

The spark of humor in Jonah's voice made her smile. She glanced around and spotted him standing in the shadows under the bar's dark green awning.

He lifted a hand and waved.

She shook her head and fought the curve of her lips. Here was the Jonah she remembered. The Jonah who made sure he got the last word and wouldn't leave until he'd put a smile on her face.

"Is that a no?"

The amusement in his words told her he was teasing. "Now isn't a good time."

"There never is. Just say yes, and I'll hang up and leave you alone. At least for now."

Jillian tapped her toe against the cracked sidewalk and blew out a shaky breath. "Fine. I'll see you Saturday." Even from a short distance, Jonah's bright smile nearly blinded her. She disconnected the call and turned to face Antonio, but he was gone. She stood on her tiptoes and leaned to the side to see past the people in front of her.

Antonio walked with hands in his pockets, his shoulders hunched forward, and the energy of a broken man surrounding him.

So much for a simple lunch.

Chapter Eleven

The hard Adirondack chair on his mom's back deck somehow curved exactly right against his spine. The gentle pull of his muscles reminded him how out of his workout regimen he'd gotten during the last couple of months. Hammering nails and moving lumber wasn't cutting it. One morning helping Dylan at his farm proved how out of shape he'd become.

"I either have to help you more often or go to the gym. Being this sore by a day's worth of work is ridiculous." Jonah rubbed the stiffness from his bicep and closed his eyes against the glare of the late afternoon sun. September might have arrived, but the heat of the sun hadn't dimmed, and the leaves had yet to change. Dylan's deep rumble of laughter threatened to shake Jonah's chair.

"I didn't realize you'd become such a pansy since you became a civilian," Dylan said.

The back door swung open, and footsteps fell across the floorboards, followed by the scratching of claws on the wooden planks. "Don't let him fool you. He's always been a pansy."

He didn't have to open his eyes to figure out what smart-aleck made the comment. Meg helped him and Dylan unload hay from Gilbert Farms into the stables for the horses. That his little sister had hauled more hay than him wounded his pride, even if he'd never admit the fact.

A few beats, and more footsteps, passed before the door banged closed.

"Don't be rude, Meg," his mom scolded.

Her voice told a story of exasperation for all the times she'd had to step into their bickering. Jonah opened his eyes and squinted. Raising a hand, he used it as a shield and grinned at his mom. Annie placed a galvanized tray with a pitcher of lemonade and plastic cups on top of the table between him and Dylan. His mouth watered, and he straightened in his chair. "Thanks, Mom."

"No problem." Annie took a seat at the four-person table beside Meg.

Nora, Meg's Australian Shepherd, picked up her head.

Annie leaned back into the plump cushions and crossed her ankles. "You should sit under the umbrella. The shady spot helps with the sun."

"Good idea, Mrs. S." Dylan poured himself a glass of lemonade and then took the other empty seat beside Meg. "So, Jonah. Everything set for tonight?"

He groaned and hoisted himself from his seat. He'd only filled in Dylan on his plans with Jillian because he needed Dylan's help to set up everything at the farm. He'd agreed to help Dylan with the chores today because Dylan lent him the barn. His mom and sister were the last two people he wanted to spill the details of his date with. "Yep." Jonah scooted into the chair across the table from Meg. The heavy metal of the legs screeched against the deck, and bells rang in his ears.

"What's tonight?" Meg tilted her head and twirled the end of her braid between her fingers.

The innocent inflection of Meg's tone told him she already knew the answer. Damn Dylan and his big mouth.

"Jillian and I have a date." Jonah lifted the red plastic cup to his mouth and let the ice-cold lemonade cool him from the inside out.

Annie's feet fell to the floor, and she clapped her hands together under her chin. "You do? Oh, that's wonderful. Where are you going? I didn't even know you two were talking again."

Meg shook her head and smirked. "Drop the drama, Mom. Everyone's talking about them. Don't act like you weren't in on the gossip."

Meg's disbelief made Annie scowl, and Jonah hid his chuckle behind a hand. His mom's main mission was to be the first one in town with the dirt on everyone.

"I don't gossip." Annie drew back her shoulders. "I might have heard some things here and there, but nothing I'd believe until Jonah told me himself." She raised her brows. "So, what are you two doing tonight?"

Her stare pinned him in place, and Jonah rubbed the two-days' growth of whiskers on his chin. He really needed to shave before he picked up Jilly. "I'm taking her to Dylan's farm."

"Seriously?" Meg snorted and hid her mouth with her hand.

Meg's laughter made his blood boil and doubt his plan. "Yes. Jillian and I have a lot of memories there, and recreating some of them would be nice." He downed the rest of his drink and avoided eye contact with anyone. Maybe his plan was stupid. He should just take her out to dinner or something.

"The place looks real nice," Dylan added and locked his gaze on Meg. "We set up things in the main barn. Cleaned out some clutter and hung some lights. You'd like it, Meg."

Jonah glanced at his best friend but couldn't gain his attention.

Meg's vibrant blue eyes sparkled back at Dylan.

Dylan broke eye contact, and his cheeks burned the same red as his beard.

What the hell?

"Meg likes dirt and jerks. Blake wouldn't know how to add a little romance if someone handed him notes on the subject." Jonah laughed, but the only sound joining him was the soft whinny of horses in the fields.

Meg tightened her jaw, and the sparkle in her eyes dimmed. Tension coated the air, and a low growl gurgled from Nora's throat.

"Dude."

Dylan's voice barely carried across the table, but the warning blared loud and clear. *Oh, man.* Jonah shifted in his seat. "Meg, I didn't mean that. I was joking around."

Meg shrugged and gave a little shake of her head. Her blonde braid bounced on her shoulder, and she traced a finger along the condensation left on the table from her cup. "I get it. You don't like my idiot fiancé. Trust me, I'm used to people having a bad opinion of Blake. Maybe if I'm lucky Emma will give me a hard time about it, too, when she gets here in a few hours." She pushed up from the table and stepped into the house with Nora on her heels.

Jonah fell back against his chair. "Shoot."

"You're the only idiot I see right now." Annie frowned and crossed her arms over her chest. "You always take things too far with her. She might want us to think she's got a thick skin, but she hides a lot. She always has."

"I'll go talk to her." Jonah set down his cup on the glass table.

Dylan's hand crushed down on his shoulder. "I got this. You've got a date to get ready for." He stomped his heavy boots across the deck.

Jonah glanced at his mom. "Since when have those two been so close?"

Annie settled back into her chair. "You've missed a lot since you've been gone. You'll need more than a month to catch up. Dylan's been a good friend to Meg. And even if I agree with you about Blake, forcing her to see the mismatch is not up to us. She has to figure out who Blake really is for herself."

Frustration turned his stomach. Meg didn't need to waste time on a man who didn't treat her right. "But he's such a tool. She deserves so much better. I'm supposed to sit back and watch her settle?"

Annie lifted her cup to her mouth and stopped, her light eyebrows barely visible above the rim. "Don't you have enough to worry about?"

Heat rose from his neck and flooded his face. His mom never minced words, and he hated how spot on she was. "I do, and right now, I need to worry about getting ready."

"Have you and Jillian talked about what happened between you two?" Annie cradled her cup in her lap.

He nodded and dropped his gaze to his clasped

hands on his knees. "We've talked."

"About?"

His mom's prying made his skin crawl with annoyance, and he unclasped his hands to scratch his forearm. "About what we needed to talk about, okay?"

"Okay."

Annie drew out the word like a bubble being blown. Jonah tensed, waiting for the next question he knew would come.

"What about her ex-husband? Is he still in the picture?"

Jonah scrunched together his face and rubbed the coarse hair above his eye back and forth. *Don't snap at your mother, don't snap at your mother.* He might have a good six inches and eighty pounds on her, but she'd still figure out how to whoop his butt if he gave into the urge to yell.

Standing, he glanced at her with the biggest smile he could muster—which, if the way his cheeks pinched at the corners was any indication, made him look like serial killer. "Jillian and I are going on a date, not getting engaged. Let's not make it a big deal. I got to run. I still need to get ready, and then stop at the farm to make sure everything's in place. I'll call you tomorrow."

He bent down, kissed her cheek, and stepped off the back stairs into the yard. The closer he got to his truck, the louder the lie he'd told his mom rang in his head. Tonight was one of the biggest nights of his life. It could be the beginning of the rest of his life with Jillian, or the end of the only dream he had left to hold on to.

****

The needle on the speedometer climbed higher and higher. The ripped leather of the steering wheel bit into Jonah's hand, and he pressed his foot harder on the gas pedal. Nerves zipped through his body and caused anxious energy he needed to get rid of. Wind slapped in from the open window and drowned out the music on the radio. Corn stalks rose high on both sides of the road and passed in a blur. At this time of year, the dry, brown husks hid everything from view.

Jonah tapped a finger to an imaginary beat in his brain, and he glanced at the neon green clock on the dashboard. He had twenty minutes to double check the set up at the farm, and then drive into town to pick up Jillian. Beads of sweat formed at his temples, and he cranked the air conditioner despite the mild temperature. Anxiety dipped so low in his stomach it almost hit the seat.

The smell of smoke wafted into the truck—not like cigarette smoke, but a campfire. An image of late nights, s'mores, and snuggling under a blanket with Jillian washed over him and eased a bit of anxiety. They had one hell of a history, and most of it was good. The best times in his life had been with her, and the good times were what he needed to focus on. The magic was still there. All they had to do was surrender to it.

Thick, black smoke swirled into the air and curled against the twilight sky in his peripheral vision. He turned down the long lane to Dylan's house, and a punch of fear took away his breath.

Orange, vibrant flames licked into the air from the barn in the middle of Dylan's property—the barn where they'd set up his date.

He stomped the pedal to the floor. Loose gravel pelted the side of his truck. He winced at every sharp ping that threatened to chip his paint. He cranked the wheel, and the truck skid toward the side of the house. Slamming on the brakes, he lurched forward, and the steering wheel jammed into his chest. Fear and adrenaline churned together in his gut, leaving him unfazed by the impact. He threw the car in Park, jumped out of the truck, and ran toward the fire.

The scorching blaze consumed the wooden walls of the barn and singed the brilliant red paint until it bled black. The wood cracked and popped. The smoke grew thicker, and the fire grew higher.

No, no, no.

Fear fisted in his gut. He had to get help. Now. He reached for his phone, but it wasn't in his pocket. Damn it! He'd plugged his phone into the charger in his truck. He raced toward his truck, and his foot slid over something round and raised off the ground. Jonah caught his balance and glanced downward.

What the hell?

He bent down and picked up a blow torch. The hot metal burned his skin, and he narrowed his gaze to study it.

The sound of approaching sirens caught his attention, and he straightened. Red lights whirled into the sky, and blaring sirens vibrated against his skull. His heartbeat picked up, and his pulse pounded in his ears, but he took a deep breath and stood tall. A panic attack wouldn't help Dylan right now. He tightened his grip on the blowtorch and focused on the heat seeping into his skin. The heat burning into his flesh was real. The pain was now.

A fire truck pulled into the driveway, followed by the blue and white lights of a police car.

Jonah stepped back to give them room to work. As much as he wanted to charge in and take action right now, he couldn't do much. He didn't even know where Dylan's garden hose was to help douse the fire. Best to let the professionals do their jobs and stand by if they had questions.

The fire truck screeched to a stop in front of the barn. Firefighters jumped off the truck and got to work.

Damn, he wished they'd turn off the siren. The scene in front of him played like a movie. The roof of the barn collapsed in spots, and the yells and the scream of the sirens drowned out the yelling firefighters.

Not knowing what else to do, Jonah took a step forward to help in whatever way he could, when a strong grip on his arm stopped him. He glanced into the hard, brown eyes of a cop.

"Do you want to explain what's going on here?" The cop nodded toward the barn.

"This place is my friend's. I'm Jonah Sheffield. You probably know my mom, Annie Sheffield. I stopped by to check on something, and the barn was on fire." Not one muscle on the weathered face wavered. No emotion displayed.

"And you didn't think to call in the fire?"

"The fire truck flew up the lane before I could get to my phone in my truck. I figured I'd stay out of the way and let them do their job." He tried like hell to keep his frustration from his voice, but the words came out tight. The slight frown on the officer's face told him he didn't succeed.

"And what about the fancy blowtorch you're

carrying?" The cop dropped his gaze to the object in Jonah's hand.

Suddenly, the heat of the smooth metal became too much to bear, and he dropped the blowtorch. "I tripped and picked it up to see what it was."

The police officer snorted, grabbed Jonah's elbow, and twisted his arm behind his back. He swiftly grabbed the other arm and clasped together his wrists.

The cold slap of handcuffs had Jonah's heart racing like a racehorse coming to the home stretch. "What the hell are you doing? I didn't do anything. This house belongs to my best friend. Dylan Gilbert. I'd never do anything like this, especially to him." Panic made his pitch rise higher than the flames still burning in front of him.

"Jonah Sheffield, you're under arrest. Anything you say can and will be used against you..."

The front wall of the barn crashed to the ground and drowned out the rest of the cop's words. But he didn't need to hear them. He was screwed.

Chapter Twelve

"We're here," Jillian called into her parent's house. She ushered Sam into the brick ranch she'd grown up in.

Sam shrugged off his jacket onto the tiled foyer floor and then ran into the living room.

Jillian's mom stepped into the foyer and chuckled. "He's just like you were as a kid. Couldn't wait long enough to get from one place to another to stop and hang up his coat."

Jillian sighed and leaned down to grab the jacket from the floor. "I swear I taught him better." A smile played on her lips. Sam's sloppiness was an ongoing joke between her and her mom. She hoped he grew out of it as she had, and sooner rather than later.

Pamela took Sam's coat and hung it on the rack in the corner of the room. "Big plans tonight? Has Antonio bought a house yet?"

"I think so. He's mentioned a house he liked, but I haven't seen it. Things have been a little tense." She opted to answer the second question and ignore the first. Her mom wouldn't be thrilled she was going out with Jonah, and the conversation wasn't one she wanted to have.

"Antonio moving back will be good. Bouncing around the way he does can't be good for anyone. Putting down roots will make helping with Sam easier.

I hope we still get to watch Sam from time to time. He sure does lighten up things for us."

Pamela's rosy checks glowed, and her grin widened, deepening the wrinkles at the corners of her mouth. Sam was lucky to have grandparents who adored him as much as her parents did. "I'm sure you'll see him plenty. Even with Antonio in Smithview, he'll still have a pretty busy work schedule." She glanced at her watch. "Sorry, Mom, but I really have to go. I won't be too late tonight."

"Wait. You never told me what you were doing."

Jillian opened the front door and shot her mom a smirk. "I know." She blew her a kiss and closed the door.

A light breeze rustled through the air, and Jillian put her hands in the pockets of her fleece jacket. She'd walked Sam to her parents instead of driving despite the cool night air. Thankfully, they were just down the street, so she wouldn't be late for Jonah. The slight chill gave the promise of fall—of Friday night football games and cuddling with loved ones to keep warm. How many high school football games had she attended to watch Jonah play? How many nights had she pretended to be cold as they sat on his porch swing just to get closer?

Buzz- buzz.

Sam must have realized he'd forgotten to tell her goodbye. She grabbed her phone and read the screen.

—*Please meet me at 352 Pine Street. It's urgent*—

Concern collided with confusion at Antonio's vague text. She unlocked her phone and punched in his number. She didn't have time to deal with games right now. The phone rang and rang. When the call went to voicemail, she ended the call and popped up her text messages.

—What's this about? I don't have time to meet you right now—

Three dots blinked under her message. He should have answered the phone when she'd called, and they could get whatever was going on figured out. Instead, the blinking dots mocked her with his incoming response.

—Please. I need you. Won't take long—

Jillian took a deep breath and prayed for patience. Pine Street was only one street over, and to drop by and see what was wrong wouldn't take long. If Antonio was in trouble, she didn't want to leave him stranded. But what was he doing there in the first place? Pine Street had nothing but single-family houses.

—Be there in a couple minutes. Can't stay long—

Every step she took brought on a new burst of irritation. Of all the nights Antonio insisted she meet him, it had to be tonight. She stomped out her annoyance, but pounding her boots against the sidewalk didn't work. She turned on to Pine Street and glanced at the mailboxes as she passed each house.

348, 350, 352...you've got to be freaking kidding me.

Stopping on the well-lit sidewalk, Jillian stared at the two-story Colonial house, and her jaw dropped. A *Sold* banner stretched across the For Sale sign in the pristine yard. She hustled up the cobblestone walkway to the front door, and her fingers trembled at her sides. She drooled over this house her entire life, but as far back as she could remember, it had never been on the market. Years ago, she had even joked with Antonio she would be willing to bribe the owners with free books for the rest of their lives if they'd sell it.

Two topiaries flanked the door, and Jillian pressed a finger to the doorbell.

Ding dong.

She aimed an ear toward the door and strained to hear anything from inside. No footsteps echoed. No voice called out.

Even if Antonio had bought the house, his recent purchase didn't explain why he needed her to come by tonight. If something was wrong, he wouldn't answer the door. Maybe she should go in. Her mind spun with possibilities, and she pressed down on the doorbell again, and then used her fist to pound on the heavy door.

Again, nothing but silence. Without wasting another second, Jillian twisted the doorknob and hurried into the house. The beautiful mahogany floors and grand, two-story foyer begged her to stop and appreciate them, but she tiptoed into the dark house. No lights burned in either room to her sides, but shadows danced toward the end of the hall. She continued down the hallway to the spacious, gourmet kitchen. Her breath caught. Not because of the large island in the center of the room or the marble countertops gleaming against oak cabinets, but because of what stood in the great room on the far side of the kitchen.

Flames flickered everywhere. They danced in the gas fireplace, the candles set up around the room, and the spark of lust in Antonio's velvety brown eyes.

He stood at the threshold between the kitchen and the family room with his hands clasped in front of him.

His thumb stroked up and down his finger,

showing his nervousness. His white button-down shirt and khaki pants showed no sign of wrinkles, which meant he'd actually ironed for once. Antonio hated ironing.

Jillian stepped in front of him and let her gaze wander around the room. Empty except for the candles, a blanket sprawled in the middle of the wood floor, and a wicker basket on top of the blanket. Confusion swirled in her mind like a dense fog, but dread pooled in her stomach. Antonio's history of grand gestures never ended well, especially when he used his actions to force her hand.

Antonio's light touch grazed her arm.

A chill raced down her spine. She glanced at him and watched as the shadows moved across his olive skin. "What did you do?" she whispered the words, afraid of how loud they'd bounce off the high ceiling.

Antonio shrugged, and his mouth morphed into a wide smile. "I bought a house. I might have greased a few palms to make things move as quickly as possible, but I need to be with you and Sam. I'm tired of crashing at Blake's house when I'm in town. We need a home we love to build our family in and move forward."

His words flew at her like spit wads off a slingshot—fast and impossible to catch. She didn't have time to process everything.

He skimmed his fingertips down her arm and intertwined their fingers. "So? What do you think?" He tightened his grasp on her fingers.

Her breathing came out in rapid pants. She froze from her inability to express the thoughts running rampant in her mind. He'd trapped her with his grand gesture, his kind words, and his large hands. Her esophagus tightened and blocked the passage to her lungs. She pulled her hand from his.

His hand didn't release.

She cleared her throat to free the airflow, but it didn't help. "I can't have this conversation right now."

The shadows across his face made his quivering chin and pinched-together mouth menacing, and he tightened his grip.

A shot of pain pierced her skin, and she yelped. "You're hurting me."

Antonio dropped her hand, took a step back, and tunneled a hand through his hair. "Damn it, Jillian. What else do I need to do? I'm trying so hard here, and you're giving me nothing. I understand we have some issues to work on, and what you said about me leaving the other day was true, but we can't get past all of our problems if we don't try. Please, just try."

Her heart palpitated in tiny flutters like the rapid wings of a hummingbird. She had to get out of here. "Now isn't a good time." She kept her voice low and calm, not wanting to upset him more.

"No time is good for you," he spat. "I'm tired of being yanked around. Tell me what's going on in your head."

She dropped her gaze and rubbed the toe of her boot across the ground. As irritated as she was, his words hit her heart like an arrow hit a bullseye. She'd asked for time, from him and Jonah, and she needed to let them know where her head and her heart were. "You're right. I need to be honest. I've spent the past weeks figuring out what I want, and I don't think you and I are a good idea."

"You didn't even try." He took a step forward and

balled his fists at his sides.

Anger heated his words, but she stood her ground. Antonio wouldn't hurt her. He loved her. He was upset, and he had every right to be. From the beginning, she should have been more honest about her misgivings—with him and with herself.

Anxiety knotted her stomach. She might not want to be with Antonio, but she didn't want to hurt him. "You and I getting back together is too complicated. We have a good thing going, and I don't want to mess it up. Our marriage didn't work the first time, and it won't work the second time. And this time we'd hurt Sam a hell of a lot more than we did before. Giving us another chance is not worth the risk."

Antonio snorted and shook his head. "And Jonah is?"

"My decision isn't about Jonah. I made up my mind based on us and how I feel."

He took another step closer until the toe of his shoe brushed against hers.

His broad shoulders blocked out the light from the flames burning around them and closed them into darkness. His hot breath brushed against her forehead, and she lifted her chin. The hunger in his eyes nearly weakened her resolve.

"Are you sure? Because I don't think I was given a fair shot, Jillian." He parted his full lips and lowered his mouth to hers.

Maybe she hadn't really tried. Maybe if she gave him one more shot, one more chance, to show her rekindling their relationship would give her what she wanted he could prove her wrong. She closed her eyes and leaned into him.

He wrapped his arms around her back and molded her to his body.

His heart thumped wildly against her chest, and his tongue pressed into her mouth. He stroked the curve of her spine, urging her to meet his frantic demands. But she didn't respond—no tingling sensations, no butterflies in her stomach, no raw desire she was desperate to fulfill. She opened her eyes and pressed against his chest.

He didn't move, only pushed his tongue deeper into her throat.

Irritation tensed her muscles. She shoved harder, and the corners of her mouth ached from his roughness. She grabbed fistfuls of his shirt and yanked to break into his trance.

A deep groan rumbled from his throat.

The vise-like grip of his mouth sealed to hers and kept her from turning her head. Panic clawed at her throat. She wanted him to stop, so why wouldn't he release his hold on her lips? She used her short fingernails to claw into his chest. She slipped a finger between the buttons of his shirt until she found skin and dug in.

Antonio jumped away and grabbed his chest. "What the hell?"

Ragged breaths tore through her, and she stumbled away until her hips ran into the island in the kitchen. Using the back of her hand, she wiped saliva from her mouth. "What is wrong with you?"

Antonio crouched to the ground and hung his head in his hands. "I'm...I'm so sorry. I thought maybe. I don't know. Maybe if I kissed you, your feelings would change." He kept his gaze locked on the floor.

His trembling voice didn't soften her anger. "Forcing yourself on me was the best way to show your feelings? I considered giving our relationship another chance, I promise I did, but that kiss only solidified my decision. You're Sam's father and a good friend, but nothing more. After tricking me to come over here and being so forceful, I don't even know if I'd call you a friend." Her hands shook at his deception.

His knees hit the floor, his gaze staring straight ahead.

Disgust swirled in her belly. She never imagined he'd resort to such low means.

"Please, Jillian, let's forget this happened."

"I don't know if I can. At least not for awhile. But I don't have time to argue with you. I told you I had plans tonight, and I couldn't stay long. You lured me here by acting like some damn emergency had happened. Are you a child?" She lifted a palm to stop him from speaking. "You know what, don't answer. I don't want to hear one more thing from your mouth right now."

She turned to leave when a soft vibration buzzed against her thigh. My God, what planet had crossed over into the night sky to completely mess with her plans? She grabbed her phone and glanced at the screen. She didn't recognize the number, but she could never let a call go to voicemail if she could help it. The call might have something to do with the store. "Hello, this is Jillian. Can I help you?"

A brief pause sounded on the phone. "Hi, Jilly. It's Jonah."

She turned her back to Antonio and glanced at her watch. Jonah was supposed to pick her up in five minutes. She never should have believed Antonio was in trouble. Now she'd be late, unless Jonah was also behind schedule. "Hi. Are you on your way? I got a little tied up, but I'll be home in a minute."

"Jilly, I'm so sorry, but I need you to pick me up."

His voice was rough like he'd swallowed a piece of sandpaper. "Okay, I'll stop by my house and get my car. Where are you?"

"I'm at the police station. I was arrested."

Jillian gasped and dropped her hand without disconnecting the call, and her body slumped in defeat. Never mind the planets aligning to mess with her night, God himself must be out to get her.

Chapter Thirteen

Jonah tightened his grip around the cold, metal bar caging him in the small cell at the local jail. The police officer who'd arrested him sat with his back toward him and hunched over his desk with a blinding lamp shining down on whatever the hell he worked on. He offered an explanation to the guy, but the cop hadn't wanted to hear a word. The officer wouldn't even let him know how much damage had been done to Dylan's property or how the fire had stared. If he was to blame by putting candles in the barn, he'd never forgive himself.

But he hadn't lit the candles yet, and where had the blowtorch come from?

Seconds ticked by and bounced off the cement walls, blaring in his ears to remind him of the time spent in a cage. Trapped. No light. No survivors.

His ragged breaths caught in his chest and refused to travel up his throat. The entombed air burned like the fire that destroyed Dylan's barn. He pressed his body against the bars, as if he could seep through the narrow slits if he tried hard enough. He shook his head and jammed his fingers into his eye sockets. Now wasn't the time to lose himself in the past. He wasn't in a tank in Iraq, listening to his friends die. He was home.

The stale smell of liquor and vomit permeated from the slumped-over drunk in the corner and brought Jonah back to the present moment. Jonah checked his gag reflex to keep from adding his own puke to the mix. He narrowed his gaze on the clock in the corner of the room and willed it to speed up so Jillian could get here and get him out of this hell hole.

The loud creak of the heavy door in the front of the square room made him whip his head around.

Jillian swept her gaze around the space until she found him. The honey highlights in her blonde hair danced around her face, and she tucked long bangs behind her ear. She smiled in his direction, and then marched to the front desk with a don't-mess-with-me expression.

Relief and embarrassment clashed inside him, leaving him nauseous. She'd shown up when he'd needed her, but he hated her seeing him behind bars like a criminal.

"I'm here to bail out Jonah Sheffield."

Her tone demanded attention.

The officer straightened in his chair. "Jillian Adams? Does your mama know you're here?"

Jillian's eyebrow lifted so high like a fishing hook latched onto the arch and yanked it toward the ceiling.

"Excuse me?" Jillian asked.

"I don't think your mama would want you spending time with an arsonist." The cop hooked a thumb over his shoulder.

Jonah resisted the urge to thrust his middle finger in the air.

The officer anchored his fists on the desk. "I don't care if he's a Sheffield or not. He's been a nuisance since he's been home. Everyone knows he knocked out Blake, the boys on Gus's crew have talked about how aggressive he gets with a sledgehammer, and now he set fire to the barn at the Gilbert farm. You're a nice girl. You don't need that kind of trouble in your life."

Anger burned so bright in Jonah's body that little spots of light burst over his pupils.

She fisted both hands on her hips. "I'm not a girl, sir, and I don't need to clear my social life through my mother. I did not come to seek your opinion on whom I spend my time with. I'm here to get my friend out of this pit. A pit he obviously doesn't belong in because he'd never do what you accused him of."

Pride expanded in his chest, pushing against his lungs and making breathing hard. Jillian had always been a spitfire, and he was glad to see she still charged to life when faced with injustice.

The wooden legs of the cop's chair scraped against the linoleum floor, and he pushed his wide frame to his feet. "Fine, but don't blame me when he takes you down with him. You were raised better."

Jillian lifted her narrow nose into the air, and the fluorescent light showed off the smattering of freckles across her face. She grabbed her wallet from her purse and handed the disgrace of the Smithview Police Department her credit card.

Officer Moron ran the card, grabbed the keys, and let him free. "Don't leave town. You'll be hearing from the courts soon. You better get yourself a good lawyer."

Jonah kept his mouth shut, grabbed Jillian's hand, and stepped outside. Anger heated the blood in his veins. The police should be searching for whoever had set the fire, not wasting time by keeping him locked in a cage.

Dusk had come, and the pale moon hovered near the horizon. The police department sat catty corner from the courthouse and on the edge of the town square. Cars crawled by, stopping at the only four stoplights in town. The streets and sidewalks were full of people searching for something to do on a Saturday night.

Hunching his shoulders, Jonah kept his head down. He ran a hand over his scraggly hair and wished like hell he had his baseball hat. The last thing he needed was witnesses for his jailhouse escape. Though he had little doubt news of his arrest would spread like wildfire around town in no time.

"My car's in the parking lot." Jillian tugged on his hand and led him to the side of the jail. "Where do you want to go? Do you want me to take you home?"

"I need to get my truck and find out what happened." If the police weren't looking into what really happened to Dylan's barn, then he'd have to find the jerk who'd started the fire.

"Okay."

Her calm voice was like a healing balm over his wounded soul, and some of the tension in his neck loosened.

They approached her car in silence, and he climbed inside. His knees crowded into the tight space, and he messed with the lever on the side of the passenger seat until he slid backward a couple of inches. "Thanks for coming. I'll pay you back tonight."

Jillian started the engine and pulled away from the jail. She lifted the side of her mouth and spared him a glance before returning her focus on the road. "I'm not worried about the money. What happened? Did Dylan's barn really catch on fire?"

Jonah leaned his head against the head rest and

squeezed his eyes shut. An image of Dylan's barn collapsing into a pile of singed rubble seared his brain. Dylan had enough on his plate right now with his dad's deteriorating health and keeping the farm running on his own. He shouldn't have to deal with his barn being destroyed on top of it. The barn catching on fire couldn't be an accident. The fire was because of him. Someone wanted him to take the blame, and only one person in this town hated him that much. He just needed to find a way to prove it. "I have an idea about what happened." The weariness in his voice must have warned Jillian away from asking more questions.

A soft melody sang on the radio, but the sound was so low he couldn't tell if the song was country or rock. With Jillian, the music was probably country. His body swayed with the gentle movement of the car. Fatigue weighed him down, and the methodic motion of the tires bouncing along the pavement lulled his muscles into a catatonic state of relaxation.

The sharp turn of the car told him they'd arrived at Dylan's. With a sigh, he opened his eyes and scooted onto the edge of the seat. He lifted his chin to get a better glimpse of what scene of devastation waited. Dust and smoke hung heavy in the still air. Soot marred the ground and covered the surrounding buildings. The massive barn that had stood in the middle of Dylan's outbuildings and stables for as long as he could remember was now a giant pile of charred wood and broken dreams.

Jillian let out a low whistle. "Holy cow."

Dylan, Meg, and Emma stood shoulder-to-shoulder-to-shoulder, watching the cinders die down. Meg's slim fingers brushed against Dylan's back.

Something nasty twisted in the pit of stomach, but he couldn't put his finger on what it was. Guilt? Anger? The desire to find who'd done this and put a fist to his face? Because even though the candles, table, and flowers would have made great kindling, something else had to have started the fire. He had to figure out what...or who.

Jonah jumped out of Jillian's car and slammed the door shut, the sound startlingly loud against the absence of birds chirping and the people he loved most in this world talking. No one greeted him, and the gravel crunched beneath his feet as he stepped beside Dylan.

Jillian's lighter footsteps fell behind him until the brush of her shoulder rested against him. "Dude, I'm sorry."

Jonah wiped a damp palm over his eyes and then slid it down to his freshly shaven chin.

"You don't have anything to be sorry about. I need to find whoever does, though. The firemen said the cops had someone at the station. They found him here right after the fire started with the blowtorch in his hands. Now that they're gone, you can bet I'm going to the station to see who's sitting in a cell."

Anger dripped from every word and made each syllable shudder. Jillian's muscles tensed against his arm. Jonah swallowed a groan and kicked the loose pebbles on the ground. "I'm the one they arrested."

"What?" Three voices shouted the word at the same time, and three faces stared with wide eyes.

Jillian laced her fingers in his.

Her touch gave him strength. He kept his gaze locked on the dying embers, unable to look in the eyes of the people who meant so much. "I stopped by to make sure everything was ready for my night with Jilly, and the barn was already on fire. I ran to my truck and tripped on a blowtorch lying in your driveway. The fire truck and a police officer showed up, and I guess I looked guilty. Jillian had to bail me out."

Dylan marched toward the farmhouse with his massive hands bulged into fists at his sides.

"Where's he going?" Emma cut her gaze toward Dylan then Jonah.

Worry coated Emma's words and Meg glanced at Jonah with wide eyes then jogged after Dylan.

Emma crossed the short distance between them and gathered him into a hug. "Are you okay?"

"I'll be fine." He cleared his throat and brushed off her concern. "When did you get into town? Where are the kids?"

Emma dropped her arms and smiled at Jillian before she answered. "We got here a couple of hours ago. Dylan was still at Mom's when he got the call. Meg and I came out with him, and I left the kids with Mom."

"Sorry you came home to such a disaster." His gaze took in the extent of the damage, and the lingering heat from the now-dead flames smacked his face. Smoke burned the inside of his nostrils, and he covered his mouth to keep it from entering and drowning his lungs.

"Would you stop apologizing?" Jillian snapped and released his hand. "You didn't do anything. Let's go inside and talk to Dylan. We'll all get smoke inhalation standing so close to this mess." Jillian wrapped her arms around herself and headed toward the house.

Emma's gaze followed her and then narrowed back

129

on Jonah. "You called Jillian to bail you out?"

He shrugged and shoved his hands into the front pockets of his jeans. "Calling Jilly made sense. She was waiting for me to pick her up."

Emma tucked in her lips and arched her eyebrows. "I like seeing you two together again."

Jonah rolled his eyes. With everything else going on right now, his almost-date with Jillian wasn't where their focus should be. "We planned one date. Don't get too excited."

"Well, that one date has turned into one hell of a night." Emma smirked and rocked back on her heels.

"Shut up. Let's go." He fought against pleasure creeping into his voice, but the excitement in Emma's eyes told him he hadn't succeeded. But the truth was, tonight might be one of the biggest disasters of his life, but it told him a lot about Jillian's feelings. She had been there when he needed her and had gone to bat for him more than once. Hope blossomed in his chest, but only for a second. He had bigger fish to fry at the moment.

Neither spoke as they approached the house. He followed Emma up the steps to the cement stoop at the back of the house, and they stepped into the mudroom off the kitchen. Jonah kicked off his shoes and found Dylan, Jillian, and Meg sitting at the large, rectangular table in the middle of the eat-in kitchen.

Bottles of beer sat in front of them, but only Dylan's had been touched. He took a seat next to Jillian on the two-person bench, and Dylan's Golden Retriever, Betsy, rested her head on his thigh. Jonah placed a hand on the top of her head, and the gentle motion of his fingers rubbing through the fur calmed his frayed nerves.

"I still can't believe they arrested you. That's so messed up." Dylan tightened his grip on his bottle and shook his head.

The paleness of Dylan's usually tanned brow stood out in sharp contrast to his dark red beard.

"What do I need to do? Call and tell them I'm not pressing charges until they find the person who really did this?"

Jonah grabbed the brown bottle in front of Jillian and took a drink. "The guy at the station said I'd get a call soon about court dates. I don't know how the process works. I need to call a lawyer tomorrow."

"Tomorrow's Sunday." Emma shoved her hand through her hair. "We can't do anything until Monday."

"Like hell I can't." Dylan slammed his now-empty bottle against the table. "I can find out who did this and kill him. The fire wasn't an accident. Someone wanted to ruin my barn, and I'll discover why."

"Why would someone want to burn down your barn?" Jillian asked with wide eyes.

Jonah put an arm around her shoulders and pulled her close to his side. "Maybe it wasn't about the barn." He didn't want to believe it, but the barn where he'd set up Jillian's date-night surprise was torched less than an hour before they planned to be there couldn't be a coincidence. "Who else knew about my date with Jillian?"

"Me and Meg. I didn't tell anyone else. I swear." Dylan shook his head and held his hands in the air.

Jonah grazed a fingertip against his chin. "Did you talk to her in person? Maybe someone overhead you."

Meg rested an elbow on the table and rubbed her

temple. "No. He called me the other night to talk about transporting the hay for the horses. I was home with Blake when we spoke."

"But Mom obviously heard things around town. Secrets are non-existent here. Someone else could have found out." The wheels in his mind spun like a hamster on speed running for its life.

"We won't figure out anything tonight." Emma stood and threw away her beer bottle. "Dylan's upset, Jonah's angry, I'm tired after driving across the state with two kids. Let's talk more tomorrow. I need to get back to the inn."

"Before you get together, do you want to stop by the store?" Jillian asked Emma. "Now might not be the best time to ask, but I'd love to get your input about décor before you go back to Cleveland."

"Don't you mean when we get together?" Jonah glanced at Jillian, and his eyebrows threatened to touch his hairline. "You're a part of figuring out what happened." Jillian's cheeks flushed the prettiest shade of pink. Speckles of yellow flared in her irises.

Her lips slipped into a smile. "Okay."

"Then it's settled," Emma said. "I'll come by the store, and then eat dinner at Mom's to figure out what to do about this mess."

Everyone nodded to Emma's plan.

She gave a wave and left the kitchen.

Jonah glanced at Jillian. "I'm sorry tonight sucked. Can I get a rain check?"

"Absolutely."

He stood and focused on Meg. "Heading home?"

Meg picked up her beer and shook it. "Gotta finish my beer first."

Jonah glanced at Dylan, then back to Meg, and shook his head. He hoisted a leg over the bench and moved into the mudroom with Jillian right behind him.

Warm fur brushed against his fingertips, and he glanced down and smiled at Betsy. "Hey, D," he called from the mudroom. "Can I take the dog home with me tonight? She seems a bit attached."

"Sure. Bring her back in the morning."

Dylan's deep voice vibrated the thin sheet of shiplap between the kitchen and mudroom.

Jonah slipped on his shoes, ruffled the top of Betsy's head, and glanced over at Jillian. Betsy might not be the woman he wanted in his bed tonight, but at least he wouldn't be alone. After a night like tonight, demons would wait to greet him in his dark, empty house. He didn't want to face the nightmares alone.

Chapter Fourteen

With all the enthusiasm of entering the dentist office with a cavity to be filled, Jillian stepped into her parent's house. She'd dropped Sam off only an hour ago. No way would her mom let her leave without an explanation as to why she was back so soon, and she was past lying about a guy.

Wasn't she?

Yes, she absolutely was. Straightening her spine, she passed the blaring television in the living room and entered the kitchen. Her mom didn't watch much television, especially whatever obnoxious cartoon blared on the forty-inch flat screen above the fireplace. Chances were, she'd be either cooking, baking, or cleaning something in her favorite room of the house.

The scent of garlic, cilantro, and seasoned meat lingered in the air and made her stomach growl. The mouth-watering smell reminded her she hadn't eaten dinner.

Her mom stood in front of the sink, her shoulders hunched forward and her back toward Jillian. The gentle swish of water echoed around the otherwise-quiet room. Jillian stood and let the simple motion of her mom plunging her arm into the water and wiping dishes calm the stupid nerves jumping around inside her. "Smells good in here. Anything left?" Forced cheerfulness coated her words, and she prayed her mom wouldn't notice.

Pamela whirled. Water splashed from the sink and landed on the floor in a pile of suds. "What are you doing here?"

Jillian kept her facial features calm. "I'm here to get Sam."

"But he hasn't been here long. What happened?" Pamela grabbed a dish towel from the counter and wiped off her hands.

Jillian sighed and sat at the same round table that had been in the kitchen for as long as she could remember. She ran her fingers over the familiar grooves in the old wood. She might as well get the conversation over with and tell her mom everything. Jonah's arrest would be all over town tomorrow anyway. "My date with Jonah's postponed because there was a fire at Dylan Gilbert's farm tonight."

Pamela covered her wide-open mouth with her hand and sank into a chair across from Jillian. "That's horrible but explains why you smell like a fireplace."

Jillian nodded and hoped her mom wouldn't ask any more questions.

A beat passed, and Pamela furrowed her brow. "Why didn't you tell me you're dating Jonah? Why would a fire at the Gilbert's farm make you cancel your date?"

Sighing, she leaned back and crossed her arms in front of her. "I didn't tell you about Jonah because tonight was our first date, and I didn't want to make a big deal. You aren't his biggest fan, and the last thing I wanted to hear was all the reasons you think I shouldn't give him another chance."

Pamela clenched her jaw, and a vein throbbed at

her temple. "But he broke your heart. You spent months getting over him—"

Jillian held up a hand. "Things happened between me and Jonah you know nothing about. I don't need a lecture, just your support."

"What about Antonio?" Pamela whispered.

Images of her earlier encounter with Antonio flashed in her mind, and she squeezed shut her eyes to block them out. For a moment she'd forgotten about the other disaster she had to clean up. "Antonio and I will remain friends and co-parents who love Sam and put him first. But nothing else is between us." Pamela's deep frown and hooded eyes expressed her disappointment clearer than any words she could have spoken. Her mom was a firm believer in keeping a family together no matter what.

Pamela wiped her fingertips against the table and arched her brows. "You know what's best for you, dear. But can you explain again why you smell like ashes, and why Jonah canceled your date? Seems to me he needs to learn how to honor a commitment and not leave you high and dry. Flakiness isn't an attractive quality in a man."

Jillian suppressed a sigh. Showing her irritation wouldn't improve the situation. "He had a good reason to cancel the date, but I don't want you to freak out when I tell you." Pamela's eyebrows threatened to collide with her hairline, and the wrinkles in her forehead deepened into small ravines.

She'd never agree not to get upset. "Jonah was arrested for setting fire to Dylan's barn, and I had to bail him out of jail."

"What?" Pamela exploded from her seat. "Are you

out of your damn mind?"

Jillian stood and faced off with her mom across the table. Indignation flared in her cheeks. "He didn't start the fire, Mother. Why would he? Dylan's been his best friend for years, not to mention he had set up our entire date inside the barn. Someone framed him, and we will figure out who."

"What's going on?" Jillian's dad stood in the doorway.

Concern etched fine lines in his weathered skin.

Pamela kept her hard gaze locked on Jillian. "Your daughter's about to make a giant mistake, and she's too stubborn to listen to reason."

Jillian threw her hands in the air. "I don't want to deal with your ignorant opinions. Where's Sam?"

Sam peeked his head around her dad and kept his gaze on his feet. "I'm right here. Let's go."

Jillian's stomach dropped to the polished tile floor. Sam's pouty frown and sad eyes ripped at her soul like the talons of a falcon tore open its prey. How much had he heard? She crossed the room, put her hands on his shoulder, and guided him to the front door. They'd talk about what he might have heard later. She couldn't handle any more drama tonight.

****

"Please tell me you won't wear that sour expression throughout dinner?" Jillian and Sam sat in her idling car in the driveway of the inn. He hadn't said more than five words since he'd walked in on her conversation with her mom the night before.

Sam leaned against the headrest with his face pointed toward the window.

He wouldn't even glance in her direction. All day

he'd tried her patience. He hadn't been happy to sit at Kiddy Korner while she'd worked and even less thrilled to stay after closing so she could give Emma a tour of the new store. But she hadn't wanted to deal with her parents today, and she wasn't ready to call Antonio. "Look at me."

Sam glanced her way, his mouth set in a tight line and his brown eyes glassy.

She widened her eyes and kept her gaze locked on his. "You will not be rude. Do you understand?"

Sam nodded, and then pushed open the car door.

Jillian said a silent prayer to help keep her temper in check before stepping out into the crisp fall air. Maybe bringing Sam for dinner wasn't a good idea, but she didn't have a choice.

The front door opened, and Meg stepped out into the wide porch.

Nora skirted around her legs, leapt off the stairs, and ran toward them with her tongue hanging over the side of her open mouth.

Sam dropped to the ground with open arms.

Nora slammed into his chest and the shaggy dog's tongue coated his face.

Jillian cringed, but his laughter kept her from making him stop. She'd make sure to wash his face before she kissed his cheeks.

"Nora's getting spoiled today. First Sophie and Anderson, and now Sam. She'll be bored when all the kids are gone." Meg descended the stairs much slower than her dog and smiled at Sam before catching Jillian's eye. "Emma's inside. She can't stop talking about the new store. She's already drawing on napkins and talking paint colors. You have no idea what you're in

138

for."

Laughing, Jillian stuffed her hands in the pockets of her light jacket. "I'm excited to hear what she has to say. Where's Jonah? I was surprised he didn't come to the store earlier with Emma." She fought the eagerness from entering her voice and chanced a peek at Sam to gauge his reaction to Jonah's name. She still wasn't sure what all he'd heard at her parent's house the night before.

Meg's gaze followed her line of vision toward Sam rolling on the ground with Nora. "My mom reached out to a friend this morning about his situation. She wanted to talk with him about his options before you two got here."

Jillian nodded her understanding. "Is he inside?"

"Jonah's in the backyard in Mom's garden. He's had a tough day. I think the fire stirred up some other stuff, but he won't talk to us." Meg glanced over her shoulder then met Jillian's gaze again. "Maybe you could talk to him? I'll stay with Sam while he helps get out some of Nora's energy before dinner."

Sam didn't stop petting Nora, and Nora didn't stop lapping up whatever she found so interesting on Sam's face.

Jillian tucked in her lips and nodded her agreement. "Sam, stay with Meg. I'll be inside for dinner in a minute, okay?"

Boy and dog both turned toward her with their heads tilted and their brown eyes glistening.

"Is it me, or do they kind of look alike?" Meg asked with a laugh. "Let's get Sophie out here, too. I have a feeling you two will get along great."

As if the mention of her name summoned the little

girl, Sophie appeared on the porch with long strands of blonde hair propped on her head in the cutest pigtails Jillian had ever seen.

Like a tiny tornado, she ran off the porch and hurled herself into Meg's arms.

Sam straightened and giggled.

Jillian rounded the side of the house, and the deep colors of Annie's garden popped against the blue sky. She hurried along the brick pathway. The urge to meander along the path and admire the colors of fall snaking their way alongside the walkway pulsed through her muscles, but she kept her focus squarely on Jonah, who stood alone at the far end of the garden. "What are you looking at?"

Jonah's muscles tightened.

She came to a stop beside him. "I'm sorry. I didn't mean to startle you."

"You're fine." Jonah stared at the ground. "I'm a little jumpy."

Jillian glanced at the ground to see what held his attention. A small, stone statue of a soldier sat in the dirt. The solider stood at attention, saluting an American flag flowing in the gentle breeze. In front of the solider a bronze plaque read; *In loving memory of Brad and Mike. Brothers by bond if not by blood.* "That's beautiful. Did you know them?" She kept her voice low and tender.

Seconds ticked by with the flapping of the flag the only sound between them. Finally, he rubbed a palm across his face. "Yes. Besides Dylan, they were the closest things to brothers I've ever known. They were in my tank when we got hit."

Her throat tightened, making it difficult to swallow

back her emotions. "I'm sorry you lost them." She took his hand.

He turned to face her, his eyes wide. "Do you know how much I'm soothed by having you by my side and holding your hand in mine? I haven't felt this much peace in years."

"You look like you could use a little peace today, Jonah. Do you want to talk about what's bothering you? I'm a good listener."

He sucked in a large breath. "I don't know. Something about the fire last night left me in a weird place. I hoped I was getting past what happened in Iraq. After I talked to you, a weight lifted from my shoulders. Then something happens, and I'm right back where I started. I'm right back in the damn tank. Having those feelings of hopelessness come crashing back is frustrating as hell."

"Healing takes time. You can't expect all of your pain and grief to vanish because of one conversation. Coping with grief isn't easy." She let out a long breath and tamed the hair blowing across her face. "And what happened last night…well, being arrested for a crime you didn't commit would mess with anyone's mind."

His arm tensed beside her. He glanced down, and tears glittered in the corners of his eyes. "I lie in bed every night and pray to finally have a decent night's sleep. At the same time, I'm scared to death to close my eyes because I know what's waiting for me. Every day I get out of bed, and I can't help but wonder why I'm still here. Why didn't I die with the rest of them? Sometimes I think it would have been better if I had."

Pain sliced through her, and she fought the urge to cringe. "Don't you ever say you should be dead, Jonah

Sheffield. No one's life would be better if you weren't here. You dying wouldn't bring them back." Her voice cracked, and her hands shook. "But you make so many lives better by being here."

"Do I make your life better, Jilly?" The tears in his eyes had vanished, and he pressed his lips in a tight line. "All this other stuff doesn't matter as long as you're by my side."

She snatched her hand from his and slapped his chest. "Of course, you make my life better."

He captured her hand and held it over his heart. "You make my life better, just by being in it. But I want more. Are you ready to give us another chance?"

Her head spun, and her heart hammered in her chest. She searched for the right words to express herself, but nothing filled the blank space in her mind. Jonah stood in front of her, and she wanted him—not like a girl with a school yard crush, but like a woman who craved the man she loved. Words weren't important right now. Showing him was. She leaned into him and pressed her lips to his.

He wrapped both arms around her waist and crushed her against his chest.

Her heart raced, and she snaked her arms around his neck. The heat of his body spread goose bumps over her skin. Her body demanded she give into her burning desire. Opening her mouth, she deepened the kiss. Her tongue invaded his mouth, probing as deep as it could. The intensity of her desire shocked her, but only for an instant.

He matched her passion by molding her to him.

She fiercely gripped his hair in her hands and groaned her pleasure into his mouth.

"Mom, where are you?" Sam's voice shouted from the side of the house.

They flew apart.

Jillian panted to steady the beat of her heart. Fever ripped through her body, flushing her face. She patted down Jonah's hair, mindful of the fact her hands just roamed through it a moment before. She hoped Sam couldn't read the guilty expressions they wore when he ran up. "I'm over here." She cleared the lust from her dry throat.

Sam followed the brick path and stopped in front of them. He narrowed his eyes first at Jonah, and then focused on her. "What are you doing?"

"I'm talking to Jonah. I thought you were playing with Meg and Nora?" The birds chirping overhead mocked the false cheerfulness in her voice.

"Dad texted me. He wants me to see his new house. Can we go?"

Sam's clipped words and harsh tone told her everything she needed to know about what Sam witnessed between her and Jonah, but she couldn't let it bother her. "We've already committed to eating dinner here and can't leave now. Doing so would be rude."

Sam sighed and kicked the toe of his sneaker against the ground. "Fine. Can we go after we eat?"

To keep her already thin patience from snapping like a rubber band pulled too tight, Jillian clenched her teeth and counted to five in her head. "No. After dinner, you need to go home and finish your homework before bed. I'll call your dad, and we'll plan a day this week to see his house." She needed to speak to Antonio anyway. Better to get the conversation over with and stop stewing over what had happened.

"Whatever." Sam rolled his eyes and stomped toward the front of the garden.

Jillian bit into her tender flesh inside her mouth and watched him go. Dinner would be unbearable with Sam now, but she needed to stand her ground. A light touch on the small of her back had her turning around. A smile lifted Jonah's full lips and understanding lightened his bright blue eyes.

Her relationship with Sam might be strained at the moment, but at least she'd finally figured out her heart. Her heart belonged to Jonah. They had each other, and the rest would all fall into place. It had to.

Chapter Fifteen

His muscles twitched, and sweat clung to every surface of his body. Blasts of light crashed against his eyelids, and screams echoed around him. He thrashed against his blanket and concentrated on opening his eyes. He couldn't. His eyes stayed closed as if someone had glued them shut in the middle of night. Now, he was forced to live in the darkness.

Jonah gritted his teeth, and a scream tore through him. His muscles ached as he strained against them, his body rigid. Finally, his eyelids lifted little by little. Slivers of sunlight broke through the dark clouds in his eyes. His body collapsed into exhaustion as the beams of light streamed in around him and pulled him back to the present.

Damn it. He ground the heel of his palm into his forehead. The nightmares had gotten better since being home, but no doubt the disaster of the last forty-eight hours played with his mind. The dreams were relentless—coming night after night to drag him back to hell. He gasped and struggled to catch his breath. Icy fingertips of dread shot up his spine.

Throwing the covers to the floor, he flung his legs over the side of the bed, dropped his head to his hands, and greedily sucked air through his nose. His lungs burned, and his heart raced. Bile slid up the back of his throat. He jumped off the bed and ran into the

145

bathroom, making it just in time. He retched up the contents of his stomach and hung his head low in the toilet.

He stood and his legs shook beneath his weight. He braced his hands on either side of the white pedestal sink. The stale smell of vomit lingered in the bathroom. He ran his tongue over his teeth and cringed. He turned on the facet and cupped water into his mouth. The water didn't help. Grabbing the toothpaste, he scrubbed his teeth until the minty flavor overpowered the acidic taste of bile.

The toothbrush slid out of his hand and fell into the sink. He used the back of his hand to wipe leftover toothpaste from his lips. He rinsed off his hand, his reflection stared back, and he cringed again. Blood-shot eyes and pale skin mocked him, and his hair stuck out in all directions. Two days' worth of stubble covered his jaw, and he rubbed a hand over his chin. Damn, he looked rough. His head spun, and dismay ate away his stomach lining. Hopefully, a hot shower would fix him up.

Hot water pulsed down on him, and he lowered his head and let the heat beat out the tension in his shoulders. He lingered in the shower until the water turned cold, and then he quickly dried himself and threw on some clothes. Water still trickled down the back of his neck as he left his house and drove into town for work.

Jonah tightened his grip on the steering wheel. He had to erase the terrifying dream from his mind. Dwelling on the fire wouldn't do him any good. He focused on evening his breath and imagined Jillian's hand in his. He pictured the freckles scattered across her nose and the way the yellow in her eyes edged out the green when desire took over. The way they'd looked last night after he'd kissed her.

He slid his truck into a spot in front of Kiddy Korner. He sat in his truck and rubbed his eyes. A large yawn clawed from his mouth, and he pressed his fingers harder into his sockets. Exhaustion weighed him down, but he had to push past the fatigue.

Tap-tap-tap.

Jonah jolted against the tattered, cloth seat of his truck, and his heart rate kicked up a few notches. He glanced out the driver's side window and into the worn and wrinkled face of Gus. Jonah rolled down the window and the cool morning air poured into the truck, sending goose bumps up his bare arms. With a cough, he cleared the sleep and the alarm at Gus's sudden arrival out of his throat. "Hey, Gus. You need something?"

"Yeah. Wanna grab some coffee real quick?"

Jonah searched Gus's hound-dog face for a sign of what he wanted, but his expression remained unreadable. "Sure." He cut the engine and climbed out of the truck.

Average Joe's stood down the street from the bookstore, and they walked side-by-side in silence. The bare sidewalks spoke of the early hour, and Jonah rubbed the chill from his cool skin. He hadn't expected to be outside, so he hadn't bothered grabbing a jacket. At this time of year, the sun would soon chase away the briskness with warm rays that beamed down and spotlighted the turning leaves.

When they reached the only place in town that served decent coffee, Jonah pulled open the door and held it for his boss. He followed Gus toward the counter.

Gus grabbed his wallet from his back pocket. "I got this. Why don't you find us a seat?"

Jonah nodded and headed toward the seating area. Although a small line waited to order from Joe, every table in the coffee shop sat empty. He took a seat at the closest, two-person table to the cash register and drummed the pad of his index finger against the tabletop. A quick glance at his watch showed him he and Gus were due to work in five minutes. What could Gus want to talk about that would make them late?

With a to-go cup of coffee in each hand, Gus's bulky form ambled toward him. Jonah stood and grabbed one, ready to head back to the store.

Gus motioned with a tilt of his chin for him to sit back down.

Jonah fell back into his chair.

Gus sat across from him, placed his palms around his cup, and dropped his chin toward his chest.

Jonah lifted his cup to his mouth, and the jolt of hot liquid on his tongue had him cursing under his breath. He waited. Gus had something on his mind, and he'd spill it when he was ready. Jonah lowered his coffee to the table and tucked in his lips while keeping his gaze locked on Gus.

"I'm just gonna spit this out. You're off the crew, son. I'm sorry to do this, I really am, but with everything going on right now, I can't afford to keep you."

"What do you mean because of everything going on?" Jonah kept his voice low. Even though the tables around them were empty, someone waiting to give their order could hear their conversation.

Gus scratched the back of his head and frowned. "I'm not saying I think you did anything wrong. But I can't ignore the rumors, or the fact you were arrested for arson. My business can't take the hit."

Jonah bit down so hard on the inside of his lip blood flooded his mouth. Anger burned hotter than the coffee in his stomach, but he couldn't let it out. Yelling at Gus wouldn't do any good. "What the hell am I supposed to do? How can I live without a job?"

"I really am sorry. I hate to see you go. You've been a real asset on this project. We're way ahead of schedule and will be done in another week. And honestly, getting let go isn't that bad of a deal for you." Gus glanced around then leaned forward. The extra layer of fat around his stomach pushed against the side of the table. "Listen to me. You've got a real talent for construction, and you're wasting it working for someone else. Take this time and get your contractor's license. When this nonsense dies down, I'll be retired, and the town will need someone to fill my shoes. I can't think of anyone better to do that than you."

"People in this town will hire someone accused of setting fire to his best friend's property?" The words flew out on a rush of contempt.

Gus leaned back in his seat and tilted his head to the side. "Did you do it?"

"Hell no!" Jonah banged a palm against the table.

"Then the truth will come out eventually, and when your name is cleared, you'll be ready to get on with your life."

Gus's matter-of-fact tone settled his turmoil over the injustice of the situation…a little bit. He'd never entertained the idea of being a contractor, but the longer it stewed in his mind, the more he liked the idea—being his own boss, having his own crew, picking his own projects. He just wished getting fired wasn't the way he'd had to figure out his next step. "I have to grab some stuff I left at the worksite." No need to argue existed. He had to collect his things and go home.

"All right. Let's go."

Jonah welcomed the brisk air against his skin on the way back to Kiddy Korner. The slight breeze and low temperatures weren't enough to cool the anger simmering in his blood, but it helped a little. Things were looking up. He enjoyed his work, Jillian agreed to go out with him, and he'd finally managed his PTSD. Now, because of some jerk's agenda, he was out of a job, and he'd already suffered a paralyzing nightmare. He had to resist the urge to ball his hands into fists or he'd crumble his coffee cup. Since it was still more than half way full, he'd end up scalding his hand.

But he still had his future with Jillian to look forward to. Their kiss from last night played in his mind, and the heat in his blood boiled from a different emotion. A stab of disappointment punctured his stomach lining. Now that he'd been fired, he wouldn't see Jillian almost every day. That day had been quickly approaching, but it sucked the day was now today.

Gus stopped in front of the glass door to the store. "Do you want me to grab your stuff so you don't have to go upstairs? The guys should be up there."

Jonah shook his head. "I haven't done anything wrong. I'm sure as hell not hiding like a coward. I'll get it. And thanks for everything, Gus."

Gus nodded and headed inside.

The sound of hammers banging descended to the door from the stairway. Most of the upstairs work was done, and the new stairway was the last major renovation to finish. The baseboards were scheduled to go in today, which probably accounted for the hammering. Gus was right. The crew was almost done here, and if what he said was true about retiring, Jonah'd have to find a new job soon anyway.

He ducked his head and hurried past the men working on the stairs. The few tools he usually left sat on the counter in the back of the soon-to-be store. He passed by the guys he'd started to make friends with and whispers floated into the air. Not one of them said a word as he gathered his things and made his way back downstairs. Clutching his tool bag in one hand and his coffee in the other, he made a beeline for the door.

"Hey. Where are you going?"

The happiness in Jillian's voice slammed into the back of his head. He stopped and drew in a large breath before turning. "Home. Gus fired me." He tried to keep any emotion from his tone, but the crack of his voice gave him away. Jillian's wide smile fell. Her long, lean legs ate up the distance between them, and her green eyes darkened with questions.

"What? Why?"

A disgruntled laugh ripped from his mouth. "Why do you think? Too risky for his business to have an arsonist on the crew."

Jillian dropped her jaw, and the skin around her eyebrows burned red.

He lifted the side of his mouth. She had changed so much in the last twelve years, but so much about her was exactly the same.

"He can't fire you. I won't allow it. Where is he?" Jillian swiveled her head from side to side.

Jonah set his tool bag on the ground and grabbed Jillian's hand. "Thanks, but leave it be."

"But firing you is not fair. You didn't start the fire."

"No, but Gus gave me some ideas for the future, and I have other things to worry about right now. Since I don't have work today, I'll call the lawyer my mom found. I need to focus on clearing my name." He dropped her hand and switched the coffee to his other hand. "Wanna grab lunch later?"

Jillian frowned. "I can't today. I need to finish the order for the shipment upstairs plus pick out all the finishing touches on the store. I have a better idea of what I want after talking to Emma. I need to get the finishing details sorted out as soon as possible if I want to open on time."

He sagged his shoulders. Calling a lawyer wouldn't take long. What would he do with the rest of his day? At least lunch with Jillian would have given him something to look forward to. He'd been fired less than thirty minutes ago, and restlessness had already set in and weighed him down.

"What about dinner tonight? I'm taking Sam to Antonio's for the night." Jillian bounced forward on her toes and batted her long lashes.

He shifted his weight and scratched the base of his neck. Their first date should be perfect, not some thrown-together plan. But what choice did he have? He sure as hell couldn't tell her no. "All right. I'll pick you up at your place at seven p.m."

Jillian leaned forward and placed her lips on his

cheek. "Perfect. I'll see you then."

He trailed his gaze after her as she made her way back to her office. His day definitely wasn't proceeding as planned, but at least he now had something to do. He had to find a way to give Jillian the type of date she deserved. A date that ended with fireworks instead of a burned-down barn.

Chapter Sixteen

Steel swam through Jillian's veins and made her movements stiff and jerky. She didn't want to face Antonio, but she couldn't keep Sam from his dad a second longer. Sam couldn't wait to see Antonio's new house, and she was desperate for a night alone with Jonah. Jillian forced down her anger toward Antonio and strode to his front door with Sam at her side. She'd drop off Sam and leave. Now wasn't the time to clear the air with her ex-husband.

Sam raced up the steps to the narrow porch and ran into the house.

The door stood open, and a moment of uncertainty had her hand hovering over the doorknob. Sam was safely inside. She could turn and leave. But that'd be the coward's way out, and she'd have to face Antonio eventually. Best to get their first encounter out of the way so anxiety wouldn't bog down her brain for the rest of the night. Besides, Sam hadn't even said goodbye before he ran inside.

"Hello?" She stepped into the foyer. The sound of a television traveled down the hallway from the family room. She slid her sneakers from her feet and padded down the hall in her socks. Dread curdled in her stomach like spoiled milk. She'd say a quick hello to Antonio, give Sam a kiss goodbye, and then get out of here.

"Mom, I'm in the kitchen. You need to see this place."

Sam's excited words reached her ears seconds before she stepped into the kitchen.

He sat on a high-backed, tufted stool in front of the island in the kitchen. "I want to see the rest of the house. This place is awesome."

She fixed a smile on her face and stopped beside him. She hadn't told Sam she'd already been here, nor did she plan to.

Antonio stood with his rigid back to them while he stirred a large pot on the stove.

"Hey, Jillian. How've you been?"

A low, gravelly voice spoke behind her. She whirled and widened her eyes at the furniture Antonio bought. A ratty recliner sat in the corner of the room and a brown, leather sofa rested against the back wall. Blake sat on a recliner with his feet propped on the footrest. He was more out of place in Antonio's family room than the random pieces of mismatched furniture.

She'd hoped her warning to Antonio would have encouraged him to make a different friend. Obviously, it didn't. "Hi, Blake." His name floated out on a breath of annoyance. Something about the guy always spiked her blood pressure.

Leaning forward, he pressed down the foot stool of the chair and catapulted himself to his feet. "Crazy about the Gilberts' barn, don't you think? I never would have thought Jonah would screw over his best friend. But I guess it shouldn't be too surprising. He's been a loose cannon since he's been home."

He drew his eyebrows together until they almost met at the top of his nose, and a smirk made the handsome, sharp angles of his face appear sinister. Jillian ground together her teeth to keep from responding to his taunt. Metal slapped against metal, and she whipped around to face Antonio.

Antonio's narrowed gaze landed on Blake, and he tightened his grip around the whisk in his hand. He flicked a quick glance in her direction and then focused on Blake again. "What are you talking about?"

Blake's casual chuckle scratched her eardrums.

"I mean Jonah set Dylan's barn on fire. He was arrested and everything. He'll go to jail for arson. Probably a good thing. A guy like that shouldn't be walking around. No telling what he'll do next." Blake leaned forward on the island and grabbed an apple out of a bowl.

A coughing fit took hold of Antonio, but he held up a hand to signal he was okay.

Sam's eyes rounded, and his mouth fell open. "Is that true, Mom?"

Jillian sighed. She'd hoped Sam would be spared the details of what happened. Why did Blake have to be such a pain? Smoothing a piece of unruly hair from Sam's forehead, she forced a smile. "Someone set Dylan's barn on fire Saturday night, and Jonah was arrested for arson, but that doesn't mean he did it."

"You're kidding me, right?" Blake's words slurred around the bite of apple in his mouth. "I heard they caught him with the blowtorch still in his hand. No way Jonah isn't guilty."

Such heat invaded her face that she was surprised smoke didn't pour out of her ears. "This isn't the time to talk about what happened." She spoke each word through gritted teeth.

Sam stared. "You were with him on Saturday night. Did you help him?"

"How did you know your mom was with Jonah?" Antonio tightened his jaw and angled his head toward Sam.

"I heard her talking to Grandma."

"Great, Jillian. Now you're talking to our son about your dates?"

Antonio's words came out on a puff of anger. Jillian pressed together her teeth to keep from lashing out. "He overheard my mother and me discussing some things. I did not talk to him about my date."

"Grandma wasn't happy you were with him, and now I know why." Sam's chin trembled, making his voice quiver. "I thought you and Dad would get back together. Why would you want to be with a bad guy instead of Dad?"

To block out the crushing weight of Sam's words on her chest, Jillian squeezed her eyes shut. Taking a deep breath, she counted to ten. She opened them again and found three sets of eyes staring at her. She zeroed in on the only one that mattered. "Sam, honey, your dad and I are friends. We've been friends for a very long time. His moving to Smithview to be close won't change how I feel about him."

Antonio snorted.

She shot him a hard look that had him turning back toward the stove before she focused again on Sam. How could she make him understand such a complicated situation? "Honey, I love you, and I love your dad, and I love the little family we've created."

Sam jumped off his stool and stared with narrowed eyes. "How can we be a family if you won't give us a chance? At least Dad's trying. You're too busy with Jonah to even care about what I want."

Pain seared her heart like a branding iron—hot, jagged, and overwhelming. She reached for him.

He jerked away. Tears hovered above his eyelashes, and he ran out of the room. His hurried footsteps pounded off the hardwood floors…and then silence.

Tension hung heavy in the room and coated the walls. Jillian's knees buckled, and she leaned onto the smooth marble countertop to steady herself.

"Look what you did. Are you happy?" Antonio blew a heavy breath from his nose and shook his head.

The pain burned the edges of her heart until they morphed into flames of anger. She tightened her grip on the marble until her fingers throbbed from the force of the hard surface against the tips of her fingers. The pale pallor of Antonio's skin and the hard glint in his usually soft eyes angered her even more. How dare he place the blame on her. "What I did? Nothing about this situation should have ever been discussed in front of our child."

Blake held up his palms, the apple still gripped in his hand.

She wanted to grab the half-eaten apple and throw it at his head.

"I didn't mean to start anything. I thought you'd be upset about Jonah. I swear."

"Shut up, Blake." Jillian didn't tear her gaze from Antonio. Blake wasn't more than a miserable ant she could smash with her toe. He didn't deserve her time. But Antonio…he should have halted this stupid conversation before it took such a disgusting turn.

"What just happened with Sam is your fault—you

and your bad decisions." Antonio stepped toward her. "How can you be so selfish?"

She snorted and fought to control the trembling in her veins. How dare he call her selfish? After everything they'd been through over the past eight years. "Do you really want to talk about bad decisions? I bet Blake would love to hear about what happened here on Saturday night. He'll have it spread all over town before morning."

Color flooded Antonio's face. "I didn't mean to upset you. I said I was sorry."

"Apologies don't mean a damn thing. Now excuse me while I go talk to my son. I'll be back in the morning to pick him up. Try not to fill his head with any more nonsense." She stormed out of the kitchen and marched down the hall. Her feet slipped on the slick wood, but she held her head high and kept right on marching.

Sam sat on the edge of the step. Tears streamed down his face.

A crack splintered her heart in two, and she crouched in front of him. "Can we talk?"

Sam sniffed his tears and held her gaze. "I don't want to talk right now."

"Okay. I can give you a little time to process everything, but we need to talk soon. I want you to understand what's going on, and you can't do that unless we talk to each other." She stood and sucked in a shaky breath. She wouldn't push him, at least not yet. "I've got to go. Have fun with your dad, and I'll be back in the morning. Are we good?"

Sam nodded.

She squeezed her hands into small fists to keep

from gathering him into her arms. He needed a little bit of space right now and to see she respected his boundaries. Leaning forward, she kissed his forehead. "I love you."

"I love you, too."

Despite the heaviness weighing her muscles, Jillian smiled. No matter what happened in life, Sam would always be her priority. She would make sure of it.

A bulk of anger, and even a little bit of guilt, slid off her tense shoulders the moment she stepped out of the house. Maybe not all the way off—especially the guilt—but enough that she could leave the crappy conversation behind her. Maybe getting out some of her anger toward Antonio was good before they patched up their relationship, but they needed to make sure Sam wasn't around the next time they fought. Living this close to each other with so many stirred-up emotions meant disagreements would happen. They needed to figure out how to resolve their differences and move on without dragging their son into the middle.

The sun hung low in the sky, and the bite of air across her face sent a spike of adrenaline through her. Dropping off Sam had taken much longer than she anticipated, and now she barely had time to get ready for her date. Picking up her pace, she nearly jogged the rest of way home.

Once inside, she vamped up her makeup and messed with her hair. She stared at her reflection in the mirror. A few loose curls added a touch of fanciness to her normally straight hairstyle. Her new concealer hid the bags under her eyes pretty damn well, and the new red lipstick didn't scream hooker the way she'd feared.

She dropped her gaze to the blouse she still wore

from work. Panic took hold of her mind. She had nothing to wear. Running into her room, she grabbed a sweater then quickly tossed it aside. How was she supposed to get dressed? Jonah could take her through a drive-thru for all she knew. Man, she forgot how difficult it could be to dress for a date.

She stole a glance at her watch—almost 7:00. Alarm rippled through her. If nothing else, Jonah was extremely punctual. She only had fifteen minutes to figure out what to wear. She grabbed her phone from her bed and dialed Catie's number.

"Why are you calling me? You're supposed to be on your hot date with Jonah."

Jillian winced at Catie's increasing volume. "He'll be here in fifteen minutes, and I have nothing to wear." She sorted through the clothes hanging in her closest— too low-cut, not low-cut enough, too mom-ish.

Catie chuckled. "I haven't gotten one of these calls in a long time."

Jillian tightened her grip on the phone. "Okay, I don't need you laughing. I need you to tell me what to wear." She yanked open a drawer and threw shirts, sweaters, and leggings onto the floor.

"Sorry, let's see. Where are you going?"

"We're going to dinner, but I don't know where."

"Simple. Wear skinny jeans with your tall, brown riding boots. Then wear your navy blue cardigan. The heavy one, so you don't need a coat. Put on one of your loose, V-neck shirts under the cardigan. The shirt under is casual and shows off enough cleavage to be sexy. Your sweater is dressy enough for dinner, but if you want to jazz it up, throw on a chunky necklace and big earrings. Voila, you're ready for date night."

She dropped her jaw. "I don't know what's more impressive. That you picked the perfect outfit so fast or you know my wardrobe so well."

"I'll take compliments on both," Catie said.

"Sounds good. You're the best. I have to get dressed before he gets here. Thanks, love. I'll call you later." She hung up and dug through her clothes. She tossed sweaters, jeans, and hangers out of her closet until she found what she wanted. After she dressed, she studied her reflection in the mirror.

Not too bad. She glanced around her room and shuddered. Sam would love to see her room so messy for a change. She grabbed a couple of shirts and put them back on their hangers.

Ding dong.

Jillian dropped the clothes she gathered from the floor. She groaned at the disaster that would have to wait until she got home and then ran to let in Jonah. In an attempt to calm her nerves, she took one big, deep breath then opened the door. "Hello, Jonah."

A smile appeared on his face.

She smoothed down her hair. Catie had been right about the outfit.

"You look beautiful."

His words floated on the subtle breeze and heat flooded her cheeks. "Thanks. You don't look too bad yourself." That was an understatement. With his jeans tight in just the right places and a simple red sweater, he was as handsome as he'd ever been. She'd have to make sure to let him know how much she liked his hair grown out.

"Ready to go?" He cleared his throat and smoothed the front of his shirt.

His voice trembled, and her nerves slowly drifted away. "I'm absolutely ready." She wasn't just talking about the date. She was ready for this new chapter in their story and ready to again open her heart to the man she had loved since she had been no older than a child.

They strolled to his truck hand in hand and walked into whatever the future held.

Chapter Seventeen

His heart stalled in his chest like an old engine. He'd waited for this moment for twelve long years, and nothing would get in their way tonight. She smiled through long lashes, but something in her eyes sent a prickle of panic through his veins. "Is everything all right?"

She drew in a deep breath and thinned her smile. "No, but I don't want to talk about what upset me. Tonight is about us. I don't want anything to take away from this moment. Not the worries on my mind or the mess at Dylan's farm. Those problems will be there tomorrow. Tonight involves just me and you and I hope to God an enjoyable evening."

He furrowed his brow and studied her. He didn't want to talk about anything else either, but he wanted her to confide in him if she'd feel better. "Are you sure?"

She nodded, and her lips curved into a wide grin. "Positive."

"All right. We'll leave our troubles for another day." He squeezed her hand, and the warmth of her fingers intertwined with his sent trickles of pleasure down to his toes. He ushered her to the passenger side of his truck, opened the door, and helped her inside before closing the door and jogging around to the driver's side. He shifted in the driver's seat and stared.

God, she was beautiful. Dryness invaded his mouth, and his pulse jumped.

"What is it?" She bowed her lips in a small pout and dipped her chin, running a palm over her shirt. "Do I have something on me?"

He expelled a small huff of laughter. "No, I can't believe we're really sitting here. I need a second to take in this moment. We haven't been together in so long, but being with you feels so normal. Like being by your side is the most natural thing in the world, and we had our last date only yesterday."

"Being together is kind of surreal, isn't it? When I found out you moved back to town, I never in a million years imagined we would be together." She waved her hand back and forth between them and a smile lifted her lips.

He lowered his voice. "What did you think would happen?"

"Honestly? I'd avoid you and be as civil as possible when we ran into each other. I never imagined you'd work on my store, and I'd see you every day."

"Are you glad things didn't go as you planned?" He waited for her answer and held his breath.

"More than you'll ever know. I never stopped loving you, Jonah. I held on to the anger and hurt for so long, I couldn't see beyond those negative feelings." She glanced down at her clasped hands sitting in her lap.

He lifted her chin with a finger. His eyes met hers. "The ghosts of our past can't haunt us any longer. We need to look ahead and stop regretting all the things we should have done so long ago." He leaned closer and gently pressed his mouth to hers. "Now, are you hungry?"

She shivered. "Starving. Where are we going?"

"Is the Mexican place we used to eat at all the time still open? I had a feeling we both might get a little nostalgic tonight. What better place to reminisce?"

"I love that idea. The restaurant's still there. Same owners and everything. Sam and I have gone few times. He loves Mexican food." She dipped her chin. "But going without you always made me a little bit sad."

"No need for sadness tonight, baby. I'm here with you now and for however long you want to keep me around." He grabbed her hand and lifted it to his lips. "Let's go."

Like always, they found limitless things to talk about as they drove. He'd always loved hearing her talk and seeing the way her mind worked. To him, she'd always been the smartest and most fascinating person in the world. He laughed at the stories she told about starting the store. He smiled when she told him funny things Sam had done as a baby. He wished he had been around to see him as the chubby little daredevil she described. Maybe then Sam would like him a little more. Her constant chatter on the way to the restaurant kept his mind off his crappy day...and the things they weren't supposed to talk about.

Jonah ushered her inside the restaurant and led her to a quiet booth in the corner. He studied the menu left behind by their server. "Do you want a margarita? Or do you want to stick with colas?"

"What does it say about me if the first drink I have on our first date is tequila?" Her eyes peered over the menu.

"It says let's get rid of the rest of the nerves so we

can enjoy our evening."

"I make you nervous, huh?" Jillian raised her brows.

His gaze bore into hers, and his pulse jumped. "You make me a lot of things, Jilly, and I think you are completely aware of what you do to me. I'm not good at hiding how you make me feel." His throat closed around the words, making his voice low and thick. He wasn't holding anything back, and she needed to know it.

"Oh boy, bring on the alcohol." She raised her menu.

The drinks arrived, and they placed their food orders.

Jillian took a drink of her margarita as soon as the server set it down. "So tell me, Jonah, what else do I make you feel?"

A shiver ran down his spine, and the muscles in his stomach tightened. "Are you sure you want to get into that here?"

"I'm a firm believer in laying all your cards on the table. Especially after what I've just experienced with my ex-husband. I'd rather know where your head is instead of finding out later."

Jonah furrowed his brow. "What did you experience with Antonio?"

She waved a hand. "I'll tell you later, I promise. Right now, I want to talk about you."

"Okay, you asked for the truth." He folded his hands on the table.

"Yes, I did." She mimicked his movements, and her gaze met his.

"When I'm with you, I'm at peace. I've been

through a lot of turmoil, and I've struggled to move on. Hard for me to feel right about moving on. But when I'm near you, a sort of calm washes over me. You're still the girl I knew so long ago, but you've also changed. You have a new side I'm getting to know. Every part of you is exactly the person I want to be with." He took a deep breath, gathering courage. "I still love you. My feelings don't scare me. Not even a little. I hope my feelings don't scare you either."

She wiped away tears pooling at the corner of her eyes and smiled. "I've waited my whole life to hear someone say those things—to hear the right man say those things. Thank you, Jonah, your words were beautiful." She took a shaky breath. "I hope the margarita wasn't doing the talking."

Jonah couldn't help but laugh. "From one sip? I hope not."

She tilted her head to the side and quirked her lips. "How can you be so sure about how you feel? About what you want?"

He shrugged. "I've never stopped wanting you, Jilly. Even after all this time. You're the reason I came home. I needed to make things right between us and win you back. Nothing in my life makes sense without you."

Jillian played with the straw in her glass. She hitched up her lip in a half-smile. "I've always had an empty space in my life without you."

"You said you've been waiting for the right guy to say what I said. How do you know I'm the guy?" He tilted her head and studied her.

She lifted a shoulder. "You've always been the right guy."

"What about Antonio?"

She leaned back in her seat and massaged her forehead "I met Antonio in college. He was a very good friend at a time in my life when I desperately needed one. One night while drinking"—she lifted her glass and made a mock toast in his direction—"things got a little out of control, and we made Sam. He was my dearest friend, besides Catie, and I figured if I couldn't have you, I might as well marry him. I owed it to the life we made to create a loving family and life. Unfortunately, our relationship didn't work."

She sipped her drink before setting it back on the table. "Antonio's living in Smithview, and having him close has been great for Sam. He adores his dad, and I love that they have such a great relationship. We've remained on very good terms with each other." Jillian sucked in a quick breath. "When he admitted he wanted a second chance, I owed it to him and to Sam to consider getting back together. But the minute you kissed me, I knew a relationship with him would never work."

Warmth trickled through him and relief loosened the knots in his stomach. Jonah grabbed her hand. He traced lazy circles over her soft skin with his thumb. "I'm glad you're giving me a second chance instead."

She smiled. "So am I."

The server arrived with their food, the scents of cilantro and garlic mingling together causing Jonah's mouth to water. He sipped the strong tequila-filled margarita then bit into his taco. He closed his eyes, savoring the sharp cheddar cheese and sour cream on his tongue.

Jillian laughed. "Does it taste as good as you

remember?"

Opening his eyes, he smiled. Wisps of Jillian's blonde hair fell across her face, threatening to stick to the salsa lingering on her cheek, and he leaned forward to tuck it behind her ear. "Honey, everything about this dinner is better than any memory I could conjure." He'd dreamed of simple moments with Jillian for so many years—moments he'd never imagined he'd have again.

When they finished eating, they lingered until the withering stares of the wait staff drove them off.

Back in Jonah's truck, he grabbed her hand again. He couldn't get enough of her, even if only the touch of her fingers on his. "Are you in a hurry to get home? Do you have to pick up Sam?"

"I have all night. Sam's staying at his dad's."

"Oh really?" He wiggled his eyebrows.

She rolled her eyes and laughed. "Don't even think about it," she warned. "We've reached an understanding about where we want to see this relationship go. Back to my empty house is not one of those places. Not yet."

Jonah clutched his chest and fell back in his seat. "You wound me. Good thing I have something else in mind for the rest of our evening."

****

The streetlights lining the sidewalks whisked by, and the dark sky opened with unobscured views. Bright stars dotted the inky sky, and the dried husks of the fall fields lined the side of the country road. Jillian tore her gaze from the window and studied Jonah. "Where are we going? My house isn't on this side of town."

Jonah laughed. "Where do you think I'm going? You don't have a lot of options around here."

She stared out her window. "We're heading toward your mom's house. Are we going to the inn?"

"By George, I think she's got it." He pulled into the long gravel driveway, shutting off the headlights as he crept behind the barn.

"What are you doing?" She glanced around and searched the darkness.

"Another stop down memory lane." He jumped down and ran over to open her door. He grabbed a blanket from the back of his truck. "Come on, hurry up, and keep quiet." He led her by the hand through the backyard and to his mom's garden.

Jillian glanced toward the house, lights ablaze inside.

Once they wound their way to the farthest corner of the garden, he stopped and laid the blanket on the ground, cradling a bottle of wine in his hand. He pulled her next to him on the blanket.

"Jonah," she whispered. "What the hell are you doing?"

He silenced her question with a quick kiss, opened the wine, and chuckled. "Well hell, I forgot the glasses. I guess we'll have to keep it classy and drink from the bottle."

"Ah, just like the old days."

He loved how the reflection of the moonlight twinkled in her eyes when she teased him.

She lifted her head to the sky. "It's beautiful here, like we're in our own little world. I've never seen the stars shine brighter."

Snuggling her close to his side, he glanced at the sky. "I forgot how much I like looking at them."

She shifted her gaze to his face. "Being here with

you is amazing."

Her voice was no more than a whisper. He caressed her face, his palm lingering on her cheek. "No, you're amazing." He leaned over and kissed her again, holding her against his body. Her mouth opened, and he probed his tongue deeper inside.

He lowered her onto the ground until they laid side by side, their mouths intertwined, gently moving against each other. He skimmed his fingers along her neck, resting on her beating pulse, and trailed his lips along the path his fingers took. They stopped at her throat, and he grinned at the rapid rhythm beating beneath them. Jillian pulled back with a teasing smirk on her swollen lips.

"Just because I said no to going to my house didn't mean I wanted you to take me somewhere else to seduce me."

"I'm not seducing you," he teased. "I'm trying to enchant you."

"Ah, well in that case, please continue."

Snuggling her close, he forced his hands to behave while his mouth rediscovered her and nibbled her ear. "Do you remember when we use to sneak here to steal kisses?" He smiled at the memory of two teenagers who had to hide from their parents in order to enjoy a little privacy.

She wiggled against him. "I still can't smell the scent of a summer's garden without thinking about you."

"Nice to know. I'll have to remember to keep fresh-cut flowers around you at all times so I'm always on your mind."

"You don't have to worry about who is on my

mind. Not after tonight."

He smoothed the hair from her face, his gaze never leaving hers. He was afraid to move or speak, as though doing so might break the spell cast upon them.

Jillian laid a hand over his. "Being here brings back so many memories. I'm happier in this moment than I ever dreamed possible. I'd resigned myself to the fact Sam was the only man I'd ever have in my life. I was happy, but being with you again is so much more then I'd ever dared to dream."

He held her close and relished the feel of her pressed against his body.

"Is someone out there?" Annie shouted from behind the screen of her backdoor.

Jillian giggled and curled against him.

Jonah placed a hand over her mouth to silence her. "Shhh," he whispered through his own laughter. "Be quiet. She'll kill me if she finds us back here."

The back door shut.

When the coast was clear, he scooped up the blanket and the untouched bottle of wine. They ran as fast as they could back to his truck. When they were safely inside, their gaze locked, and they burst into hysteric laughter. For a second, Jonah was transported back in time when he was just a kid with the girl he loved without one damn care in the world. He just hoped he could keep her by his side always.

Chapter Eighteen

Their laughter faded, and Jillian leaned back into the soft material of the seat as they headed for town. The night had been perfect, and she dreaded the date ending and returning to an empty house. She studied Jonah's profile. Moonlight poured through the window and illuminated his full lips and sculpted jaw line. How many nights had she lain awake praying for his safe return? How many days had she cried over the love who'd abandoned her?

He was here now and that's what mattered. Their past was behind them, and their future lay wide open. A light squeeze on her knee cleared the lingering cobwebs of their past from her mind.

He glanced toward her before returning his focus on the empty road ahead.

Her neighborhood passed by, and she straightened. "Where are we going now?"

Shadows shrouded most of his features, but she could make out the slight curve to his lips. He'd always loved to surprise her, so she shouldn't be shocked their date had some unexpected twists and turns.

Jonah parked his truck in front of Kiddy Korner.

She twisted her torso toward him. "What are we doing here?"

Jonah shut off the engine and faced her. "I wanted to see your expression when you see the place finished, but being here when you see it for the first time isn't an option now. By coming here tonight, at least you can tell me exactly how you envision the new store so I can experience your dream with you."

Her heart melted quicker than an ice cream cone on a hot day. Damn Gus for firing Jonah for no good reason. Jonah had been a part of constructing her store since the beginning, and he should help bring the store together in its final stage. "I'd love that."

The streetlights burned down on the empty sidewalks. She ran toward the door, and leaves rustled around her feet. A subtle chill lingered in the air, and she fumbled with the lock to the door.

Jonah covered her hand with his. He turned the key and opened the door to the deserted store. "I've never been inside when no one is here."

The red glow of the exit sign above the front door cast an eerie light around the room. Jonah pressed the pads of his fingers against her back to usher her inside.

His touch branded her skin. She flicked on the lights and shed her jacket, leaving it with her purse on the coat rack beside the door. "I'm not here by myself often. If Phyllis isn't here, then Sam is."

Familiar creaks and groans of the old store rumbled through the quiet room and Jonah took her hand. In the past few days, she felt like Jonah was drawn to a magnet in her palm. When they were alone, the only time his fingers didn't take hold of hers was when it was physically impossible. His need to be near her reminded her of their younger years when they couldn't last a minute without one simple touch.

He led her to the staircase, and she smiled. Who was she kidding? Even now she yearned for one simple touch from Jonah. But one touch wouldn't satisfy her for long.

Jonah turned on the light at the top of the stairs.

The enclosed stairwell had been opened and the once scary-as-hell flight of stairs had been transformed into a beautiful staircase that led to the large, vacant room upstairs. Tools scattered around the subfloor, and dust from the newly hung drywall coated the air. She darted her gaze around the room. Saliva filled her mouth, and she swallowed hard to force it back down her throat. "Coming up here makes me anxious."

Jonah nestled her in front of him and wrapped his arms around her waist. He nuzzled her ear. "Why?"

His hot breath caused prickles of excitement to trickle down her spine. She leaned into him and closed her eyes. Drawing in a deep breath, she inhaled his scent. "So much needs to be done. I don't have the time or the money for the renovations to go over schedule."

He chuckled. "Gus is ahead of schedule. Trust me, once the crew lays the carpet and paints the walls, not much else needs doing. He'll probably be out of here by the end of the week."

Butterflies dive-bombed against her stomach lining, but she wasn't sure if it was due to anxiety over her yet-to-be-finished store or Jonah's hard body molded against her. "I hope you're right."

"Come here." He stepped away and led her to the front of the stone fireplace. "Tell me what you want to do here. Where's everything going?"

Cool air washed down her back at the vacancy of his warmth. Jillian rubbed her cheeks with her palms. Describing her store was the last thing she wanted to do right now. "We don't have go over the details of the store."

"Please, Jilly. I want to see the room the way you do."

Jillian shrugged and turned away. No way could she think straight with that sky-blue gaze burning into her. "I want to put a couch right here." She gestured toward the empty space facing the fireplace, and excitement built like a fire from kindling. "I'll put a coffee table in front of the couch, and one chair will be beside it, kind of at an angle. Another chair will go closer to the fireplace."

He shifted his weight to the side and buried his hands in his pockets. "I can see the setup. A nice place to relax with a book, without looking like a typical waiting room or coffee shop."

"Exactly." She bounced on her toes. "I'll put some magazines and books on the coffee table so people know they're more than welcome to sit and read. I bought a big basket for blankets to put between the chair and the couch. I want people to feel like they're at home, like they can kick up their feet and snuggle in for a good read."

"Sounds cozy."

She glanced into his eyes. His eyes were like two blue pools of water. She could swim in those pools for the rest of her life.

He bent down and took her mouth in his.

Pulse racing, she wrapped her arms around his neck and pulled him closer.

He tilted back her head, deepening the kiss.

The meeting of lips soon became an invasion of tongues, breath, and life. The sweet taste of his mouth touched her tongue. His heat invaded her and warmed her to the core. She trailed her hands down his back, savoring each thick bulge of his muscles. Hunger for him roared inside of her. His tongue licked into her, and her nerve endings buzzed with life as she melted into the hard wall of his chest.

Jonah released her lips and glanced from under a furrowed brow.

Her heart pounded in her ears. She couldn't speak and took a step back, her gaze never leaving his, and nodded. She wanted to be with him...now. She loved this man with her whole heart and had no reason why she shouldn't show him. Grabbing his hand, she gathered him close to her body, and he lowered her onto the floor. Dust and debris coated the room, but she didn't care. She had Jonah in her arms, and he was all that mattered. Her and Jonah and the love they shared joining them together as one.

Jillian rested her head in the crook of Jonah's arm and turned to study his handsome face. Her heart pounded in her chest, and hope for a future she thought she'd lost blossomed, taking root in her soul.

He tugged at a strand of her hair and kissed her cheek.

Her bones melted. All she wanted was for this moment to last forever, even if sawdust clung to her sweat-dampened skin.

Bang-bang-bang.

Gasping, Jillian sat up, and panic seized her breath. The harsh interruption echoed up the stairs, but the distance couldn't hide the urgency of the banging. "What's that?"

Jonah jumped to his feet and smoothed the bunched sweater, flattening the material against his stomach.

Stomp-stomp-stomp.

Jillian scrambled up beside him and smoothed her hastily thrown-on T-shirt. "Someone's coming up here."

He stepped in front of her, and his body went rigid.

"Oh, come on, guys. Seriously?" Meg turned her back and tapped the tip of her canvas sneaker against the floor.

Jillian bristled, and heat scorched her neck and cheeks. Embarrassment and annoyance clashed together, but annoyance won out. Meg had the nerve to be irritated with them after she broke into her store and barged in? She stood tall and fisted her hands on her hips. "What are you doing, Meg?

Meg turned her clenched jaw and hard eyes toward them. Stray hairs escaped the long braid cascading over her shoulder, and the skin above her eyebrows flared bright red.

Jillian pinched her brows together and glanced at Jonah. Meg was furious, but what did Meg's anger have to do with them?

"You need to see what I found." Meg thrust forward her hand and nodded toward the phone gripped in her palm.

Jonah snatched the device. "You track us down and scare us to death to show us something on your phone?"

Meg pinched together her lips. "I tried to call both of you, but neither of you answered. Trust me. You want to see this message."

Jillian patted the back of her jeans in search of her phone, but it wasn't there. "I left my phone downstairs in my purse. Is something wrong?"

Jonah glanced at the phone for a second before he whipped up his head, and his wide eyes locked on Meg. "What…is…this…message?"

His enunciation of each word caused a shiver of apprehension to run down Jillian's spine. She leaned over his shoulder and glanced at a screenshot of a text conversation between Antonio and Blake. Antonio initiated the conversation.

—What did you do?—

—I took care of your problem. How about a little thank-you?—

—You told me you would make sure Jonah didn't make his date with Jillian. You didn't tell me you had the guy arrested for arson—

—You didn't need to know—

Jillian lifted her gaze toward Jonah. A vein bulged between the cords in his neck and even the normally white scar slashed across his red cheek. A lead ball formed in the pit of her stomach, and she swallowed the bile creeping up the back of her throat.

What had Antonio done?

Chapter Nineteen

"How did you find this text?" Jonah's blood pumped through his veins with an intensity that threatened to rip them at the seams.

"Blake stopped by my house earlier. He's been acting strange the past few days, so I looked through his phone when he was in the bathroom. I found these texts, took a screenshot, and sent it to myself."

Anger radiated so brightly from Meg's closed fist and clenched jaw that she didn't even flinch at the mention of snooping through her fiancé's phone. Things must be pretty bad between them if Meg had sunk that low. She wasn't one to get caught up in drama or resort to childish behavior. In this case, Jonah was glad she had.

Jillian trembled. "I'm so sorry. I can't believe he would do that."

Her slight tremors vibrated against his body. Jonah had to strain to hear the soft words from Jillian's barely parted lips. He thrust the phone toward Meg then grabbed Jillian by her shoulders, turning her to face him. "You have nothing to apologize for." Thick tears coursed over her high cheekbones. He wanted to strangle the jerks who'd brought this nightmare to his life even more.

"But if I had been honest sooner with Antonio about my feelings, he wouldn't have gone to such extremes. He wouldn't have…" She dropped her gaze to the floor.

The hairs on Jonah's arms stood on end. "He wouldn't have what?" Silence crackled louder than any bomb that haunted his memories.

Meg took a step forward. "Jillian, did Antonio hurt you?"

His sister's voice was so soft, so tender, that he wanted to wrap his arms around her for her compassion toward the woman he loved. But he needed to concentrate on Jillian and what had made her hesitate.

She shook her head. "He didn't mean to."

The tips of his fingers dug into her flesh.

Wincing, she tightened her muscles.

"I'll kill him." He dropped his hands into fists at his side. "What did he do?"

She lifted her gaze to meet his. "He tricked me into going to his house the night of the fire. He kissed me, and when I pushed him away, he wouldn't let go."

Her tear-filled eyes ripped a hole in his soul. Red fireworks of anger exploded in his vision. "He what?" He needed to know how far Antonio had taken things so he could justify how many times he would slam his fist into the jerk's face.

Jillian sucked in a deep, shaky breath. "I handled the situation, and Antonio's behavior toward me isn't the issue we should focus on right now. Meg, did you tell Blake what you found?"

"No, I wanted to speak with you two first. I didn't want to confront him by myself." Meg wrapped her arms around her stomach.

"Where's Blake now?" Jonah gritted his teeth, and his jaw ached.

Meg shrugged. "I don't know."

He drew back his shoulders, straightened his spine, and glanced at Jillian. "Is Antonio home?"

She nodded.

"At least I can get my hands on one of them." He squeezed his fists tighter.

Jillian placed a hand on his arm. "He didn't start the fire. Blake did. The message indicates Antonio didn't even know what Blake had done."

Jonah yanked his arm from her and narrowed his gaze. Anger made his heart pound against his ribcage. "I can't believe you're defending him. He encouraged that psycho to get between us. He used Blake to keep you from me. If not for him stalling you from going on our date, the barn would never had been set on fire. He's as much to blame for the fire as Blake."

He marched down the stairs, and the footsteps scurrying behind him bounced off his brain. Jillian's words fueled the need to make Antonio pay for what he'd done. Damn her for sticking up for him. He opened the door to the store, and cool air slapped at his face as soon as he stepped outside. He quickened his hurried pace, spurred on by his hatred of the man who tried to keep him away from Jillian—of the man who had hurt Jillian and schemed to burn Dylan's barn to the ground and have him be blamed.

The shouts of Jillian and Meg grew quieter the farther away his long strides took him. He turned onto the street Antonio lived on and said a silent prayer of thanks for small town gossip. A prayer he'd never imagined he'd utter. Everyone talked about how Antonio bought the most sought-after house in Smithview. Lucky for him, Antonio's house was only a block from the store. His anger only grew by the time he reached the front door. He lifted his closed fist and banged so hard against the door pain shot up his forearm and the wood threatened to splinter.

The door swung open, and Antonio's pinched-together face hovered in the doorway. "What the—"

Jonah pulled back his fist and smashed his knuckles into the soft cartilage of Antonio's nose. Warm blood sprayed onto his hand, and he pulled back his elbow to hit him again.

"Dad? Who's there?" Sam's voice drifted through the open door from behind Antonio.

Jonah dropped his hand to his side.

"Jonah!" Jillian yelled.

Her strained voice blasted from behind him as she and Meg raced up the sidewalk.

Antonio cupped his nose with his hand, but blood seeped through his fingers. "Sam, stay inside. Jillian, take him to the kitchen. He doesn't need to see your boyfriend assault me."

The nasally tone of his voice, along with the satisfying crunch when his fist connected to his nose, told Jonah Antonio's nose was most likely broken.

Jillian rushed passed him and into the house.

Thank God she intercepted Sam before he reached the entryway. The kid already hated him. Seeing the aftermath of Jonah hitting Antonio would only make it worse, even if he had every right to smash in Antonio's face.

Meg stopped beside him, her breath coming out in sharp puffs. She straightened and stared at Antonio. "Do I get to take a shot next?"

"Are you two insane?" Antonio stepped onto the

front stoop and slammed the door behind him. "You come to my house, interrupt my evening with my son, and assault me. Then your crazy sister has the audacity to ask if she's next? You Sheffields are something else."

Jonah took a step forward. The metallic smell of blood invaded his senses and threatened to take hold of his mind, but he couldn't let the memories take control. Settling matters with Antonio was too important. "So, you can assault Jillian, but you can't handle someone your own size coming at you? What kind of man are you?"

Antonio dropped his hand, and blood ran freely down his face. "I never assaulted Jillian. I would never hurt her."

"Really? You didn't lure her over here and force yourself on her?" He kept his voice low but couldn't stop the menace from coating his words.

Jillian stepped outside and closed the door. "I told you I took care of what happened with Antonio. We need to discuss the fire Blake set."

Antonio's face turned ghost-white. "I never told him to do a damn thing."

"Then the text messages I read between you two must be about another fire, another Jonah, and another Jillian. What are the odds?" Meg stepped forward and held her phone for Antonio to see.

"All I wanted was a chance to talk to Jillian. I overhead you two on the phone, and Blake said he'd take care of everything. I had no idea he'd do something so stupid." Antonio put his blood-stained palms in the air.

Jonah snorted. "Maybe you didn't realize what an

idiot you were dealing with, but it didn't stop you from going along with the plan. You were more than happy to let me take the blame."

"I didn't find out until earlier tonight when Jillian dropped off Sam. I swear." He tore his gaze from Jillian and sneered at Jonah. "Not that I'd do anything to help you. You're a bigger jerk than I thought. Showing up at my house to teach me a lesson about how I treat Jillian after what you did."

Confusion battled against rage. "I didn't do anything but love her. I always have."

"Oh, I know all about your past." Antonio took a half-step forward. "Did you really think she wouldn't have told me, the man she married, about everything that happened?" Fury dripped from Antonio's words and made his body twitch. Jonah fought every instinct not to step back.

"You loved her, huh? Is that why you left her alone when she was pregnant with your child?" Antonio jabbed a finger toward Jonah's chest. "You left her alone to deal with the consequences of your actions. She went to hell and back because of you, and I won't stand by and watch you hurt her all over again."

Emotions whirled around inside the pit of his stomach. What the hell was Antonio talking about? He left town as a boy with a broken heart because Jillian refused to tell him goodbye, and then never wrote to tell him what happened. She'd never said a damn thing about being pregnant. She would have told him if he fathered her child. He spoke slowly, and his voice shook with anger. "What are you talking about?"

"Jonah, please. Don't listen to him. Let's talk later." Jillian grabbed his arm.

For once, her words didn't sway him. His gaze stayed locked on Antonio.

Antonio rocked back on his heels and laughed.

As he fought not to pound Antonio into the ground, Jonah tensed every muscle in his body.

Antonio curled his lip and shook his head. "Don't act like you don't know you left to go play war hero after you got Jillian pregnant. Who does that?"

Rage vibrated through his body. Antonio had to be lying. Jillian wouldn't keep something so important from him. His hands trembled. "I don't know what you think you'll gain by spreading ridiculous lies, but I suggest you shut up." He finally glanced at Jillian. Her haunted green eyes stood out in sharp contrast to her pale face.

She scooped her long hair over a shoulder and combed her fingers through the strands over and over again.

Reality crashed down. He closed his eyes, and his knees buckled. Dread dropped in his stomach. How could she keep his child a secret? His chest tightened, and he bit into the soft flesh inside his cheek. Blood pooled in his mouth. He concentrated on the tinny taste as it coated his tongue in order to keep his shock from paralyzing him. He had a child he'd never known about.

He cleared his throat. "We need to talk. Now." His rough words were for Jillian, even though blackness clouded his vision, and he fixed his gaze above her head. He couldn't look at her. Not knowing where else to go, he stepped off the stoop and marched to the sidewalk. No neighbors loitered in the yards, and no pedestrians passed on the quiet street. Not like he would have cared. A stranded sidewalk under a strobing streetlight was as private as they would get.

His heart pounded in his chest. He stood with his legs apart and feet firmly planted in the ground. Shaking his head, he waited for words to come. Her wide eyes and puckered brow made him shake with anger, but he didn't need her concern. He needed the truth. "Were you pregnant when I left for boot camp?"

She stepped toward him and opened her mouth.

All he heard was the hoot of an owl in a nearby tree and the cacophony of questions in his own head. "Answer me, damn it." Heat scorched his cheeks.

She dropped her gaze, and tears splashed down on her shoes.

In an instant, everything fell into place. Her odd behavior before he left for boot camp, her anger toward him when he arrived back in town, and how hesitant she'd been to lower her guard. The truth crashed on him like a tidal wave. "Oh my God, Antonio's telling the truth. What the hell, Jillian? How could you keep our child from me? I had a right to be there for my baby." Pain tore through him, and he doubled over and clutched his stomach. He took deep breaths in and out, waiting for the nausea to go away.

Jillian bit her bottom lip. "I wrote you a letter. I told you I had something I needed to tell you. I didn't want to tell you about the baby in a letter. I waited for you to come home, or write me back—something. But you never did." She dropped her chin.

The slight tremble in her words didn't sway him. He snapped his head up and narrowed his gaze. "Where's my kid?"

Jillian lifted her head slowly, her hair fell into her

eyes, and she placed a hand over her mouth. A sob escaped her throat. "I lost the baby."

Pain sliced through his heart, and he inhaled sharply. "How do I know you're telling me the truth?"

She lifted her gaze and sucked in a shuddering breath. "Why would I lie?"

"You've lied for twelve years. Why start telling the truth now?"

Her head reared back. "I never lied, Jonah." She placed a hand on his arm.

Her touch scorched his skin, and he yanked away his arm. "You've never lied to me?"

She raised her chin and shook her head as tears pooled in her eyes. "I'm sorry."

A thickness settled in his throat and constricted his airway. He choked out a breath and willed the unshed tears in his eyes to stay. He wouldn't cry in front of her. "You're sorry? That's all you have to say for yourself?"

She stepped toward him, and her voice quivered. "I tried to tell you about the pregnancy the night you told me about Iraq. You didn't want to hear what I had to say. You said we had no reason to rehash the past, and we should leave it behind us."

A stab of guilt slid through him, but he brushed away the unwanted feeling. She had no excuse for keeping such a big secret. Throwing his words in his face caused his anger to flare even brighter. He held a hand up to stop her. He couldn't stand here and listen to any more of her garbage. "You should have tried harder."

He had to get away—away from her, away from Antonio, and away from the life he'd finally thought he'd found. Everything was based on one big lie. His entire body shook. He closed his eyes and counted to ten while he stomped back to his truck. The shaking didn't stop. Maybe he'd been wrong to come back and think he had a future here. One thing was clear. He didn't have a future with Jillian.

Chapter Twenty

Numbness swept through her body like water flooding a basin. The lack of feeling started at her feet, coursed up her legs, her torso, then engulfed her whole being. She wanted to run after Jonah and explain everything, but the numbness stole her ability to move. But damn it, it didn't steal the pain or the soul-crushing heartbreak Jonah had managed to inflict upon her for the second time in her life.

Her gaze stayed fixed on his retreating form—shoulders hunched, quick pace, broken man. Her vision tunneled, making him smaller and smaller as he walked out of her life.

A light touch on her arm brought her back to the moment, and she turned to stare into Meg's soft blue eyes. Meg was always the outspoken champion of everyone in her family, and Jillian braced herself for the verbal assault that was no doubt to come.

Instead, Meg wrapped her arms around her.

Jillian melted into her comforting embrace and fixed her gaze on the darkness. The events of the evening were all too much. First, the revelation about Antonio and Blake. Then, Jonah finding out from Antonio about the pregnancy and walking out of her life...again. But this time she couldn't fall apart. She wasn't a terrified teenager. She had a son and a life, and she had to keep herself together until she could hide in her room and mourn the loss of the only man she'd ever loved—for the second time.

"Are you okay?" Meg asked.

Meg's hand rubbed circles in between her shoulder blades like a mother comforting a child. Jillian sniffled and pulled away. She wiped the moisture from her cheeks and searched Meg's face for any signs of anger or disappointment. "No. I ruined everything. I should have made him listen when he first came home."

"That's ridiculous, and we both know it." Meg brushed a piece of hair from her face and jammed her hands in her pockets. "If Jonah was determined not to listen to what you had to say, no one could have changed his mind. Not even you."

Jillian shrugged and glanced down the sidewalk for a glimpse of Jonah, but he was gone. He'd walked right out of her life. Dryness invaded her mouth, and pressure pushed against her chest. Meg was right, Jonah could be as stubborn as a mule, but she should have tried harder to tell him the truth.

"Jillian, look at me."

Wrapping arms around her stomach, Jillian tore her gaze from the emptiness in front of her and back to Meg.

"I'm not worried about Jonah right now. I'm worried about you. Is what Antonio said true? Were you pregnant when Jonah went to boot camp?"

Jillian sucked in a large breath, and the cool air stung her dry throat. "Yes," she whispered. After so long without telling anyone about her past, the admission was hard to make. But the cat was out of the bag, and speaking the truth released a little ball of tension that had always existed inside.

"What happened?" Meg took a hold of Jillian's hand and squeezed.

"I miscarried." The admission was like a punch in the gut. Jillian's voice trembled, and Meg's dark pupils crowded out the blue of her eyes with barely contained grief.

"Oh, Jillian. I'm so sorry."

Jillian nodded, even though the weight of the past hour made the motion hard as hell, as if her head weighed more than her shoulders could carry. "Thanks." Hurried footsteps barreled toward her, but she didn't have the strength to turn toward the sound.

"Jillian!"

All the grief and sadness and heartbreak vanished at this sound of Antonio's panicked voice. Anger rushed to take their place. The sound of pounding footsteps hurled toward her.

Antonio ran toward them.

Worry etched deep ravines into the normally smooth lines of his face. He should be worried. She would do more damage to his pretty face than Jonah. "I can't believe you told Jonah I was pregnant. Haven't you done enough? Or you just couldn't stop until you made sure I would never be with Jonah?" Hysteria made the pitch of her voice so high it would have pierced the eardrums of any unlucky dog nearby.

Antonio stopped in front of her. His hair stood out in wild waves and dried blood matted his face.

She shoved his hard chest to make him go away.

His fingers circled around her wrists.

Not caring if his tight grasp burned her skin, she kept ramming her hands into him.

Meg grabbed her arm and yanked. "Let go of her,"

she shouted.

Antonio's gaze never wavered from Jillian. "Stop and listen. Sam's gone. I went inside and can't find him anywhere. Did he come out here?"

All the air left Jillian's lungs, and every muscle in her body froze. *No*. Sam couldn't be missing. The lie had to be one of Antonio's ploys to get her to forget how he'd ruined her life. Sam had to be inside.

"Sam never came outside." Meg glanced around. "Are you sure he isn't in the house?"

Antonio shot Meg a quick glance, and he tightened his grip on Jillian's wrists. "I'm positive."

Puffs of breath caught in her throat as it closed and blocked her airflow. She darted her gaze around the dark yard, as if Sam would appear from behind the bushes or run around the corner from her sheer desperation. He'd been shaken up when she'd gone inside. The banging on the door scared him, and she was forced to confirm Jonah punched Antonio. She didn't explain why but told him to stay put and they'd discuss it later. "Does he have his phone?" The words croaked out of her mouth.

Antonio's frown deepened, and he shook his head. "No. It's in the kitchen."

She pinched the bridge of her nose and racked her brain for where he would have gone.

"Would he have called you?" Meg asked.

Jillian reached for the phone in her back pocket, but it wasn't there. She hadn't collected it from her purse before they left the store. She glanced behind her. *The store!*

"Maybe he went to Kiddy Korner? Or back to my house?" Hope sprang to life in her chest. Antonio lived close to both. Sam probably wanted to escape the commotion and went somewhere more familiar than Antonio's new house.

Antonio nodded. "I'm sure that's where he is. Let's go." He took one step around her.

"Wait." Jillian grabbed his arm and stopped him. "What if he returns? I'll go to my house. Meg can stop by the store. We didn't lock the door when we left. Antonio, go inside and call the police. Tell them he's missing and wait and see if he comes back."

"I can't wait around and do nothing." He ran a hand through his hair, stopping at his scalp to pull the wild strands.

"Trust me, you've done plenty already." She glanced at Meg, who nodded, and she took off for her house.

Jillian quickened her pace to a sprint. Sweat broke out on the back of her neck, and a vise of fear tightened her chest. She pushed all unwanted thoughts of what could happen from her mind. Smithview was a safe town, and chances were Sam would be found soon and everything would be fine.

But what if... No. She wouldn't go there. Everything would be fine. Everything had to be fine.

The muscles in her calves screamed as she pushed herself past her normal exertion. Her feet ached as the heavy boots she wore slapped against the concrete step after step, but she kept going. She reached her front door and turned the handle. Locked. Maybe Sam locked the door after he'd gone inside. After banging on the door, she dropped to her knees to find the spare key hidden in the mouth of the ceramic frog by the door. She yanked it out, shoved it into the knob, and ran inside, glancing around. "Sam! Are you here?"

Nothing but silence and an empty house greeted her. She ran down the hallway, flipping on every light on the way, and halted outside his bedroom door. Nothing but Sam's usual mess was inside. She dropped onto his bed and buried her head in her hands. Claws of panic threatened to take her under, but she had to keep her tears at bay. She had to find Sam.

Ring-ring-ring.

The house phone blared from the kitchen. Jillian ran to answer it on time. She yanked the phone from its charger and placed it against her ear. "Sam? Is that you?" Her pulse pounded so loudly in her ear she had to concentrate to hear the voice.

"It's Meg. He's not at the store."

Jillian sank to the floor and leaned her head against the hard wood of the island behind her. "This can't be happening." A beat of silence hung heavy on the line.

"Did you call Antonio? Maybe he has more ideas of where Sam could be."

Jillian shook her head, even though Meg couldn't see her.

"What about your parents' house? Did you call them?"

Why hadn't she thought about her parents? Jillian straightened. "Oh my God, no. I have to go." She hung up before Meg could reply and pounded in their home number. How stupid could she be? Her parents' house should have been the first place she looked.

The phone on the other end didn't even ring once before her mom picked up. "Jillian? Where in the world have you been? I've been calling your cellphone, and no one will answer."

The sharp edge of her mom's voice told Jillian how upset her mom was. "Is Sam there?"

"Yes. He said Jonah punched Antonio, and everyone was yelling. What have you gotten yourself into now? To act so poorly in front of your son? Really, Jillian."

Jillian released a deep breath and let go of all her pent-up fear. Sam was safe, and knowing he wasn't harmed was what mattered. Not having the strength to argue right now, she ignored her mom's reprimand. "Keep him there. I'm coming." She hung up and called Antonio. She didn't bother with a greeting when he answered. "Sam's safe. He's at my parents' house. I'm on my way to get him now."

"I'll meet you there."

"No," she said with as much authority as she could muster. "I can't deal with you right now." She hung up without listening to his explanation or apology or whatever excuse he had. She didn't care. Pushing herself to her feet, she stared at the keypad on the phone and tried to remember Meg's number. It was no use. Her brain was mush right now. She dialed the store, and when no one answered, she called Jonah. He could pass along the message to Meg.

Her stomach muscles clenched. Each ring was like a stab to her heart. Jonah wouldn't answer her call. His voice mail picked up, and she left a brief message.

Adrenaline coursed through her veins, and she reached her parents' house in record time. She needed to get more cardio. Hell, any workout at all would have kept her from huffing and puffing after running a measly block. But she'd worry about her lack of stamina later. Right now, all she wanted was to wrap her arms around her son then figure out how not to strangle him for doing something so stupid.

She jumped up the front stoop and flung herself into the house. "Sam!" She called from the foyer.

"I'm right here."

Sam's meek voice whispered from the living room. Tears blurred her vision, but she clamped together her teeth to keep them from spilling over. She barreled around the sofa, dropped in front of him, and gathered him into her arms. One hand circled around his waist while the other snaked into his hair to check for any signs of damage. She pulled away but kept a death-grip on his arms.

Tears stained his cherub cheeks, and his wide-eyed gaze flicked from her, to her mom, and then to her dad.

"What were you thinking running off? I've never been so scared in my life." Jillian struggled not to raise her voice, but she couldn't stop the wave of fear that gripped her soul and made her words quiver.

Sam dropped his gaze and shuffled his bare feet back and forth. "I'm sorry."

Jillian tucked her fingers under his chin and forced his eyes to meet hers. "Honey, you can't say sorry and expect me not to demand answers. I need to know why you ran away. Your father and I were terrified something awful happened." Sam's eyes narrowed and gave her a glimpse of the teenager she'd soon be dealing with.

"I'm sure he was afraid Jonah would hit him again." Sam snorted.

Jillian winced and dropped to the floor. She hated how Sam witnessed his father being hurt, but she couldn't exactly tell her son she wished she could have done much worse. "I told you we would talk about what happened, but you ran off before I had the chance." A hand squeezed her shoulder, and Jillian glanced at her mother.

"Should he really be hearing this, Jillian?" Her mom lifted her brows and pressed her lips together.

"You all should. Jonah was upset because he found out who started the fire at Dylan's place." Jillian stood and faced off against her mom.

Her mom's eyebrows rose. "We already know who set the fire, dear. You just don't want to admit it."

Harsh words wouldn't help anything. Jillian swallowed down an ugly reply. "I already told you Jonah didn't set the fire. Tonight, we found out the culprit was Meg's fiancé."

"Why would he burn down Dylan Gilbert's barn? And how did you find out?" Her dad pushed down the foot rest of his recliner, set his newspaper on the end table, and leaned forward with elbows on his knees.

"He did it to help Antonio." Jillian dropped her gaze to Sam and ran a hand over his soft hair.

"What?" Sam shook his head and widened his eyes. "You're lying."

The muscles in her stomach knotted. She gave Sam her full attention. She didn't want to get into the details, but Sam deserved to know the truth. "Your dad didn't know Blake would set a fire. He wanted a chance to talk to me before I had dinner with Jonah that night, and things got a little out of hand. You have nothing to worry about, okay?"

Sam nodded, but his lips remained frozen in a frown.

"I need you to go into the guest room for a minute

while I talk to your grandparents. Promise me you will stay there until we're done speaking."

"I promise." Sam hung his head and shuffled down the hall to the guest room.

Jillian waited until the soft thud of the door closed before she faced her parents. "I'm sorry you were dragged into my mess, but thank you for watching Sam until I got here. I still can't believe he ran away."

Her mom crossed her arms and tapped an index finger against her bicep, a scowl fixed on her face. "Maybe you need to ask yourself if spending time with Jonah is worth pushing away your son."

Her mom's words broke through the fatigue pulling at every inch of her being. She couldn't listen to her criticism of Jonah anymore, which meant she had some things she needed to explain. If she wanted them to see the man Jonah had become, she had to tell them the truth from all those years ago.

"We should sit." She sat on the couch and waited for their full attention. Her chest tightened, and she cleared her nerves from her dry throat. "I never told you everything that happened with Jonah when he left for boot camp. I should have, but I was young and stupid, and I didn't know how to handle the mess I'd found myself in. But I have to tell you now, even if Jonah and I are done, because you need to stop placing all the blame on him for how I fell apart after he left." She took a deep breath and dove in before she lost her nerve.

Soft whimpers wafted from her mom's open mouth, and her hand trembled in Jillian's.

Her dad sat in his chair, eyes glassy and face flushed. Then he shot to his feet and towered above her.

She flinched but only for a second. Straightening her back, she forced herself to meet his gaze.

He leaned forward and pulled her into a fierce embrace. "I love you, Jillian. I'm so sorry you felt like you had to keep your pregnancy secret."

Emotion clogged her throat, and she squeezed her eyes.

"Both of you come here." Her mom held her arms wide.

Jillian burrowed into her mother's arms and savored the closeness. A lightness settled over her. Why had she waited so long to tell them the truth? Why hadn't she fought harder to tell Jonah? Why had she let the sin of the past rear its ugly head and crush a future she'd always dreamt of?

On a sigh, she broke from the embrace, and the emotions of the day weighed her down like heavy chains. How had a day beginning with such excitement for what the future held end with her longing for a dream that would never come true? Just when she thought she could have it all, fate stepped in to show her once again that her life didn't include Jonah.

Chapter Twenty-One

For the second time that night, Jonah made his way down his mom's driveway, and gravel crunched under his tires. Only an hour passed since he'd been here with Jillian, but his whole life was changed. Parking, he cut the engine to his truck and jumped out. He slammed the door, and the noise cut the quiet night. A blanket of clouds blocked the moon and shrouded him in darkness. For once, he didn't care. The black night matched his mood. He needed to talk to someone about the bomb Jillian dropped. He'd left Meg at Antonio's house, and Dylan had enough on his plate. His mom was the only one left to vent to.

Buzz-buzz-buzz.

He grabbed his phone from his pocket. Jillian's home number flashed across his screen. He tightened his grip around the phone until the plastic might crack. Indecision tore through him. Maybe he should answer it.

Buzz-buzz-buzz.

No. His body stiffened. She'd lied. She'd kept the knowledge of his own flesh and blood from him, and then treated him like a leper when he'd first returned to town. And why? Because she was too embarrassed to tell him the truth, and she blamed him for their failed relationship? No other explanation for her behavior existed. He declined the call, turned off his phone, and shoved it into the front pocket of his jeans.

Jonah stormed into his mother's house. Fury sparked through his nerve endings. "Mom, are you here?" His voice boomed throughout the house. "Where the hell are you?"

Annie rushed into the foyer from the kitchen. "I'm right here, Jonah. What's going on? Is everything okay?"

Wrinkles creased the corners of her eyes. "No, everything's not okay." He ground together his teeth. "In fact, everything is very, very wrong."

"Are you hurt?" She ran her hands around his face and over his arms, pushing down her lips in a frown.

"I can't believe her. She has no excuse for what she did." Annie flapped around him like a mother bird and searched for God knew what. He brushed away her hands. "Stop it." His voice came out harder than he'd planned, but he couldn't stop his anger from oozing to the surface.

Annie sighed. She rested a hand on his arm and squeezed. "Why don't you come into the kitchen and get some tea? Then you can tell me what happened."

"I don't want a damn cup of tea," he shot back. His pulse pounded against his veins. "What I want is to go punch that ex-husband of hers again, and then forget any stupid idea I had of getting back together."

"Where are your manners? First, you come barging in here, yelling at the top of your lungs, without a care if I have guests." She threw her hands in the air and shook her head. "Then you curse and keep me from getting the tea I was in the middle of making before I was so rudely interrupted. I don't care how upset you are, you know better than to act so rudely. Now shut your mouth and follow me into the kitchen." Annie turned down the hall, shoved open the swinging door to the kitchen, and disappeared.

Jonah dropped his jaw. Why had he come here? She'd make sure he told her every detail of what happened tonight. Damn it, he should have gone to Dylan's. He still needed to tell him about Blake. Stepping into the kitchen, he found his mom sitting at the table with two cups of hot tea and a plate of cookies. He shook his head. She knew him so well. No matter how much turmoil boiled in the pit of his stomach, he could never turn down one of her cookies. He took off his jacket, threw it over the island, and sat. He dropped his head in his hands.

"Are you ready to tell me what you stormed in here for, or will I have to drag it out?"

"No dragging necessary. Give me a second. My initial steam is gone after being scolded by my mom."

Annie let loose a hoot of laughter. "I haven't put you in your place in a while, have I? I won't lie…it felt kind of good."

"Humph." He grabbed a cookie off the plate, holding it in both hands and studying it for a minute while he gathered his thoughts. He took a bite and gooey chocolate melted on his tongue, then he let the rest of the cookie fall to a napkin his mom set on the table. "I finally found out what happened all those years ago with Jillian."

Annie lifted her teacup and sipped. "Oh, really?"

"Yep." He shifted the cookie around the table like a hockey puck, and his heart pounded in his chest. He couldn't believe Jillian had kept such a big secret. "She was pregnant."

Annie's cup slipped from her fingers and fell to the table. Tea splashed down the front of her sweater and onto the table, and porcelain crashed on the floor. She shot from her seat. "Oh no."

Jonah stood and grabbed a towel off the cabinet. "Jeez, Mom. Are you okay?"

She grabbed the towel and dabbed the front of her shirt. "I'm fine, sorry." She shooed him away from the porcelain. "I'll get the mess later. Sit and tell me what you're talking about. Jillian was pregnant?"

He heaved a heavy sigh through his nose and sat. He leaned back in the chair, stretched his legs in front of him, and rubbed his temple. "I had no idea. She never told me a damn thing—not then and not until just now."

Annie set down the towel and sat next to him. She leaned forward and grabbed his hand. "What happened to the baby?"

"She had a miscarriage." He cleared a hard lump of emotion from his throat. "At least, that's what she told me."

Annie furrowed her brow. "Why in the world do you think she would lie?"

Fresh rage coursed through his body. "Because she's not the person I thought she was."

Annie lifted her shoulders. "Did she tell you why she kept the pregnancy secret?"

He shook his head. "Her secrecy doesn't make any sense. I would have been here for her... Maybe things would have been different. Maybe..." He dropped his chin and bit into his cheek to keep the moisture in his eyes from spilling over.

"Oh, honey. Nothing you could have done would

have saved the baby." She patted his hand. "These things happen."

"I've lost more people in my life than I can handle, and I now I discover I lost a child I never knew about. How much is one man supposed to take?" His voice cracked, and he fisted both hands in his unruly hair.

Annie stood and stepped behind him. She wrapped her arms around his neck and gathered him close. "I'm so sorry, Jonah. You've definitely had your share of heartbreak, but you've survived and come out stronger. As much as your heart hurts, you'll get through it. And you have so many people who love you to help you along the way. Jillian's already been through her grief. I'm sure she'd love to help you get through yours."

His chest tightened. Yanking away, he twisted his head to stare. His pulse pounded in his ears. "I don't want anything to do with Jillian."

"I know you're upset right now, and you have every right to be. But you two were kids who didn't know how to handle your problems. Jillian suffered a loss as well. You can't possibly hold that against her." Annie pulled the ends of her brows together.

A cascade of wrinkles rippled across her forehead. Why did his mom always have to play the peacemaker? All he wanted was someone to listen, not solve his problems. "Like hell I can't. She didn't tell me about my baby, and then never confessed what happened after we got back together. She lied to me. I never should have come back here." He pushed his feet to the ground to stand.

Annie clamped both hands on his shoulders, shoving him back to his chair. "So because things aren't going the way you wanted with Jillian, you think the rest of us are useless? You can just leave us in the dust? Your commitment to the family makes a mother feel really good."

He twisted and lifted his gaze to meet hers, pressing together his teeth. "You don't understand."

Annie lifted an eyebrow and pursed her lips. "Then you better explain it."

He closed his eyes and pinched the bridge of his nose. This whole evening was a nightmare. He opened his eyes and winced when he spotted moisture clinging to his mom's lashes. "I didn't mean I don't need you and Meg, but I came back for Jillian."

Annie tilted her head.

Jonah blew a hard breath through his nose and shoved a hand through his hair. "You know I love being closer to you and Meg, but I wanted Jillian to be my future." He struggled to speak over the lump in his throat. "I thought…never mind, it's stupid."

"Oh no, you don't. I want the whole truth." Annie crossed her arms over her chest.

"I thought she could help me with my issues. Her face entered my mind so many times when I was in trouble. Her constant presence in my thoughts had to mean something." Betrayal burned his veins. He shrugged and hardened his jaw. "I was wrong."

Annie sat beside him and frowned. "You can't expect Jillian to be the only person to help you."

Slumping low in his chair, he sighed and shook his head. "What I wanted from Jillian doesn't matter now."

"Yes, it does. You need to find a way to help yourself, son." She rested a hand on his forearm. "Jillian can't play that role for you, and expecting her to isn't fair. The rest of us offered to be there, and you've denied needing help. No matter what the future holds for you and Jillian, you better figure out what you do need."

He blinked as fast as he could and sniffed. He rubbed his chest to erase the pain encased there. Anger, grief, and disappointment brewed together until he almost burst. His mom was right. He and Jillian might not have a future, but he still needed to get his act together. A lifetime stretched ahead, and he didn't want to feel this bad anymore. He needed to get help.

The front door slammed, and heavy footsteps pounded down the hall. The kitchen door burst open.

Meg stormed into the room. "You selfish jerk. You need to answer your damn phone when I call you five times in two minutes." Wisps of wild hair escaped her braid and flew around her face. She marched to him, her sneakers crunching on the broken glass still on the floor and shoved hard at his chest.

"What the hell is your problem?" Jonah demanded.

Meg's chest puffed in and out as she caught her breath. Unshed tears shone in her eyes. "Why didn't you answer your phone? Did Jillian call?"

"I shut off my phone. I don't need to hear any more of her excuses." He narrowed his eyes at his sister. "I can't believe you of all people would take her side."

"She didn't call to talk about your argument, you idiot. She called about Sam. Give me your phone." Frowning, she held out her hand.

He pulled his phone from his pocket and slapped it in her palm. He didn't know what was going on, but her tone brooked no argument.

"Is everything all right?" Annie straightened and bounced her gaze from Jonah to Meg.

Meg turned on the phone and waited for it to fire up. "What's your password?"

"All ones."

Lifting a brow, Meg snorted. "How creative. You have a voicemail from Jillian. Do you want to listen to it, or do you want me to?"

Irritation pulsed through him, and he fisted his hands at this sides. "What is going on?"

Meg pressed a few buttons and held his phone to her ear. She sank into the chair beside him and closed her eyes. "Oh, thank God. She found him."

"Found who?" Jonah pounded a fist on the table. "Damn it, Meg. Tell me what happened."

Meg opened her eyes.

The fire that sparked from them threatened to scald him.

"Sam ran away."

His gut twisted, and he leaned back in his chair. He might be mad at Jillian, but he didn't want the boy to get hurt.

"I went to the store to see if he'd gone there while Jillian ran to her house. I called her at home when I didn't find him and asked if she'd checked her parents' house. She hung up the phone, and I haven't heard from her since." Meg pursed her lips and narrowed her eyes. "She called you and left you a voicemail, but you were too busy stewing in your own problems to bother to answer the phone."

Jonah ached to call Jillian, but he forced down the natural instinct. "She found him? Is he okay?"

Meg snorted and tossed his phone on the table. "No thanks to you."

Annoyance crawled over his skin, and he threw his

hands in the air. "What could have I done? Don't burst in here and act like I'm the bad guy because you're mad at Blake and upset about Sam."

Annie stepped between them and swiped the broken glass under the table with her slippered foot. "Wait a second. Why is Meg mad at Blake?"

"I didn't get a chance to tell you what Meg found tonight." He pinched the thick skin on his forehead. A headache pulsed in his skull with the repetition of a hammer striking a nail...*thud-thud-thud*. "Meg found a text message on Blake's phone. He set Dylan's barn on fire because of some bizarre scheme with Antonio to keep me away from Jillian. Joke's on them. She screwed up our relationship by herself."

Annie fluttered a hand to her heart and leaned against the table. "Meg, did you talk to Blake? Has anyone called Dylan?"

Meg shook her head. "No. Things got a little intense when we talked to Antonio."

"Intense?" Jonah snorted. "My life gets blown to hell and you call it intense?"

"Would you shut up?" Meg rolled her eyes. "You're not the victim here—at least not the only one. Take a minute to feel sorry for yourself, and then get over your pity party."

Jonah rose from his chair and gripped the edge of the table. "I find out my girlfriend was pregnant with my child, and I'm supposed to get over my pity party? Screw you, Meg."

"Jonah!" Annie shrieked. "Don't talk to your sister like that."

Meg put both forearms on the table and leaned toward him. "I'm not downplaying your feelings,

Jonah. What you found out is a shock and discovering you lost a child is horrible. But Jillian didn't do anything wrong. She lost a baby and grieved for her child alone when she was barely older than a child herself."

"She should have told me." He spoke through clenched teeth.

"Maybe if you gave her a chance to explain you'd learn more about what Jillian went through. Now, if you'll both excuse me, I'm calling Dylan. He deserves to know what happened, and yet again, you're too caught up in your own problems to think of anyone else but yourself." Meg stood.

She marched out of the kitchen as quickly as she'd entered—like a hurricane, causing mass destruction without a single worry as to who her words hurt. Jonah clenched his jaw. The pain in his head intensified, and he fell back into his chair. Her words might hurt, but only because too much of what she said rang with the truth.

Chapter Twenty-Two

Late morning sunlight streamed in the window of Jillian's office, and the noise of the busy store pounded inside her head. Tension burrowed behind her eyes with the intensity of a groundhog digging a new home. She pressed the tip of a finger into her socket to ease the pain, but the pressure didn't help. The large migraine pills she'd swallowed when she'd pulled herself out of bed this morning hadn't dulled the ache either. At this point, her only options were to sleep or use a knife to take out the eye. Jillian couldn't do either while sitting behind her desk at Kiddy Korner.

She rested her head on her desk. God, she wished could stay in bed and sleep away the pain. Hell, she wanted to sleep away the whole day, but hiding in her room wasn't an option. Sam needed to go to school, Kiddy Korner needed to be opened, and she needed to get on with her life—with or without Jonah Sheffield. If she could survive the morning and make sure the paint colors on the walls upstairs were exactly what she wanted, she could escape back to bed until Sam arrived home from school.

"Jillian?"

The hairs on the back of her neck stood on end, and goose bumps tickled her skin. She didn't want to see him now. Not here, where things were crazy, and she had a ton of work to deal with. Not here, where she couldn't yell and scream about how miserable he'd made her life. She lifted her head and glanced into his rich, brown eyes. "Hi, Antonio. What are you doing here?" Her words were clipped. She didn't have time to speak with him, and she sure as hell didn't want to hear his lame excuses.

"Can we talk?" He clasped together his hands in front of him and furrowed his brow.

She gestured toward her open door. "Now isn't a good time. We're swamped."

"You can't avoid me. We need to clear the air." He pressed together his lips and ran his hand through his hair. "Please, Jillian, give me a minute."

Frustration simmered in her veins. "Would you like me interrupting you at your job? How about if I boarded a flight during pre-check?"

Antonio winced.

She sighed. Better to get this conversation over with. "Fine, you've got five minutes. Close the door before you sit."

Antonio did as she asked, then sat in the chair in front of her desk, leaning his elbows on his knees. "I'm here to apologize, and you're not making it easy."

She arched an eyebrow and pursed her lips. Annoyance and anger burned across her cheeks, singeing her ears. "And what exactly are you apologizing for? For breaking up Jonah and me? Maybe you want to say sorry for running your mouth and making me look like a liar. Or are you sorry for the fire you had Blake start to keep away Jonah, and then refused to tell the truth so Jonah would take the fall? Your antics got a man arrested, Antonio."

He dropped his forehead onto the tops of his

fingers and sighed, fixing his gaze on the floor. "I'm sorry for all of it." He lifted his head. "I wanted to protect you."

She rolled her eyes, and pain stabbed her temples. "Why does everyone think I need protecting? I'm the one who caused harm. I kept a monster of a secret. I'm the one who messed up."

Antonio cleared his throat. "I didn't exactly help. I swear to God, I didn't know you hadn't told Jonah about the miscarriage."

"I tried to tell him when he came home. I thought he knew, or at least guessed after what I wrote, but apparently I was wrong." Jillian rested her elbow on her desk and laid her cheek on a fist. Antonio was the last person she should have this conversation with, but he was here and she needed to make things right. His eyes searched hers and all of his pain and regret shined back. Her anger deflated a tiny bit. "I know you didn't mean to cause such a mess."

He snorted a laugh. "You got that right." He leaned back in his chair and chewed on his thumbnail. "Are you okay?"

Unshed tears burned her eyes. "Not really, but what can you do?"

"I can talk to the police about what really happened. I'll show them the text and tell them about my conversation with Blake. I should have listened when you warned me." He dropped his hand to his thigh and pinched his jeans. "When he said he'd make sure Jonah didn't make it to your date, I never imagined he'd go so far."

"Why would you attempt to keep us apart in the first place? And the scene at your house? Damn it,

Antonio, I'm still so angry."

Antonio slumped his shoulders forward, and he dropped his gaze to his fingers resting on his knees. "I've made a complete mess of things, and I have no excuse. I knew you'd never give me another chance. I was never the one you wanted."

His words pierced her heart, and her anger deflated like air escaping a balloon. Guilt gnawed at her conscience, and she glanced away from the hurt melting in his chocolate brown eyes. She'd never loved Antonio the way she had Jonah, not like that love had done her any good. Jonah left her with a broken heart twice, and now she'd done the same thing to Antonio. She'd never given Antonio the type of love—and marriage—he deserved. Now she needed to get past everything and make sure the last couple of weeks of miscommunication and stupid decisions didn't ruin their friendship.

Jillian reached her hand across the narrow desk palm up and gestured for Antonio to take it.

He lifted his hand and placed it in hers.

She closed her fingers around his smooth skin and smiled. "You are the one I want always to be in my life as my friend and as Sam's father. Nothing will ever change what you mean to me. I hope you stay in Smithview, regardless of what's happened. Sam loves having you here, and you and I will get past our anger."

Antonio pulled back his hand and nodded then settled into his chair.

A beat of awkward silence wove between them like a pesky cat weaving between a pair of legs—unwelcomed and unwanted but damned if she knew how to get rid of it.

Antonio cleared his throat. "Have you talked to Jonah?"

She shook her head. "I don't know if he'd listen if I tried."

"Hmm." Antonio leaned forward to cup her cheek. "You'll be fine. If you need me, you know where to find me."

Her heart stalled. "I was serious before when I told you what happened with Jonah didn't affect how I feel about you. Even if he'd never come home, you and I would never work." She kept her voice stern. They'd made progress today, but she didn't want him to misinterpret the situation. His small smile deepened his dimples and pulled at her heartstrings. She hated hurting him. He was a good man, just not the man for her.

"I meant as a friend. I don't have a lot of those around here." He stopped at the doorway and glanced over his shoulder. "I'll see you around."

The door closed.

She dropped her forehead to her desk and shut her eyes. Her headache pulsed with renewed force. Relief mixed with her anguish. Clearing the air with Antonio lifted some of the weight anchoring her shoulders. Being angry with him wouldn't solve anything, and he hadn't intentionally set out to ruin her life—or Jonah's.

No, she couldn't blame him. She had made the mistakes, and now she would live with the consequences. At least by Antonio offering to speak to the police about Blake and the fire, Jonah could move on with his life unscathed—even if it wasn't with her. A hard lump formed at the base of her throat, and she swallowed hard to push her breath past it.

Tap-tap-tap.

She groaned. Now what? The door opened, and she lifted her head. She fought to keep her mouth closed, and prickles of anxiety danced in her stomach.

Annie stepped in and closed the door behind her. "Do you mind if I sit?" She nodded toward the empty chair.

Jillian cleared her throat and licked her dry-as-dirt lips. "No, not at all." She focused her gaze on Annie as she sat down in the chair and folded her hands in her lap. "Can I do something for you?"

Annie smiled and tilted her head to the side. "No, but I hope I can do something for you."

"I don't understand." She lowered her gaze and smoothed a pile of papers on her desk.

"Jillian, honey, please look at me."

Annie's soft tone brought the tears she'd fought all day to the corners of her eyes. She didn't have the strength for this conversation today—not after her fight with Jonah last night, Sam running away, and then her conversation with Antonio.

Regretting her action, she lifted her gaze and met Annie's kind and understanding crystal blue eyes. Moisture hovered over Annie's light lashes. Emotion swam thick in Jillian's throat and made the ball lodged there moments before bigger. She pressed her tongue to the roof of her mouth and took slow, shallow breaths in through her nose. Apprehension tickled her spine.

Annie placed her hand on hers. "I wanted to tell you how sorry I am about what happened after Jonah left for boot camp." She swallowed hard. "I wish you'd talked to me. I would have been there for you. I would have found a way to tell Jonah."

Jillian lifted the corner of her mouth in what she hoped was a small smile. "I needed to tell him, Annie. Letting Jonah know I was pregnant was my responsibility, not yours. I wrote to let him know why I hadn't made it to your house before he left for boot camp. I should have said more in my letter."

"You were a kid and scared out of your mind. I could have helped." Annie squeezed her hand then leaned back in her chair. "Your parents were probably furious with us and assumed we'd left you out to dry. We all love you so much, honey. We would have been there for you."

Jillian slid her hand from under Annie's. Her heart pounded in her chest. "I didn't tell my parents about the baby until last night."

Annie gasped and pressed fingers to her lips. "Why not? Who did you tell? Who helped you through everything?"

She lifted her shoulders and bit the inside of her cheek. "I wanted Jonah to be the first to know, and I wanted to tell him in person. He didn't deserve to find out he'd be a father in a letter."

"Oh, honey. I'm so sorry."

"You have no reason to apologize. You didn't know. I'm the one who kept the pregnancy a secret. Looking back, I made the wrong decision, which made my life so much harder. I had so many people who loved me and would have helped me, and I didn't give them a chance."

Annie took a deep breath and opened her mouth. No words came out, and she pressed together her lips. She darted around her gaze, and then settled on Jillian again. "I didn't come here to talk about Jonah. I want to apologize and tell you how much you mean to me. I didn't want you to doubt my feelings because of what's happening between you and him. But I can't help myself. Did you tell Jonah any of this?"

As emotion clogged her esophagus, she shook her head and sniffled. She couldn't hold back the tears much longer. "He didn't give me a chance. He was so angry. Then I called about Sam, and he wouldn't answer the phone. He doesn't want to talk, Annie."

"Have you reached out today?"

"No," she whispered. "He made it perfectly clear he doesn't want anything to do with me."

Annie frowned and twisted together her hands in her lap. "Don't you think he deserves to know what happened?"

Indecision tore through her. He did deserve the whole truth, but she didn't know if she could face him. Seeing him might break her. "How am I supposed to tell him if he won't listen?" Her voice cracked, and she dropped her gaze to her clasped hands.

"You have to make him listen. He might be more receptive than you think. I'm not saying telling him what happened will fix everything, but he needs closure with this, Jillian. And something tells me you do, too." Annie stood, held up her hand in a wave, and then walked out the door.

Jillian held her breath and waited for another knock. When it didn't come, she slumped low in her chair and sighed. What did she expect? Jonah to burst in next to tell her he'd had a change of heart and wanted her back? Jonah would never change his mind, and she'd better put away that silly fantasy for good. She made sure the final chapter in their book was written.

Annie was right, though. Jonah deserved to know the whole truth. She couldn't turn back time and make things right, but she could move forward with honesty and put them both on a better path. Her nerves danced, and her heart clenched in her chest. Telling him everything wouldn't be easy.

Chapter Twenty-Three

The white pattern on his ceiling morphed into flowers, and then fireworks the longer he stayed in his bed. What was the point of putting stuff on the ceiling? Why not leave it flat and white, with no stupid patterns taunting the mind of whoever was forced to stare at the ceiling night after night? He rubbed his temples and sighed.

He needed to talk to Dylan. After his conversation with his mom last night, he'd been too drained to call him. Now two items needed discussing—the jerk who burned down Dylan's barn and asking Dylan how he'd recovered after returning home from war. Jonah threw a hand over the side of his bed, and the back of his hand connected hard with his nightstand. Pain shot up his arm. He closed his hand over his phone and lifted it above his face. With a tap, he brought up his contact list, pressed his finger on Dylan's name, and held the phone to his ear.

Dylan answered on the second ring. "Hey, man. What's up?"

"Are you home? I need to stop by and talk about some stuff." Jonah sat on the edge of the bed and rubbed the sleep from his eyes.

"About the fire? Meg called last night and told me. I can't believe Blake would stoop so low. If it wasn't for Meg, then I'd have gone into town last night and beat him to a pulp."

"How was Meg?" He was still mad at his sister's reaction to the bomb Jillian dropped, but he was concerned about how Blake's involvement in the fire would affect her. He didn't want her to get hurt. But maybe learning the truth would open her eyes to the kind of man she'd agreed to marry. Maybe she'd get the hell away from him before it was too late.

"She was pretty worked up when she called. Didn't say much except about what Blake did. She said she needed to calm down and would come over this morning."

Great. Another run-in with Meg, but he supposed seeing her was for the best. "I guess I'll see her there. I need to grab a shower, and I'll be over in a few." Better to get their issues out of the way than let his emotions stew.

Thirty minutes later, Jonah climbed the steps to the wraparound porch in front of Dylan's farmhouse. Cold air nipped his nose and brushed against his cheeks.

Nora ran ahead of him, turning in circles and barking in front of the door.

Meg was already here.

He grabbed the rail and sat on the top step. He needed a few more minutes before facing her. Pushing his impending exhausting encounter with Meg from his mind only allowed Jillian to slip in. Anger surged through him every time he thought of her withholding the baby. The deep weight of loss crushed his chest, and he hung his head in his hands.

A cold nose burrowed under his fingers, and Nora lay down at his feet. The door squeaked open, and heavy steps made the floorboards dip.

"Hey, man. I heard Nora barking and figured you were here. What's going on?" Dylan squeezed onto the top step.

Jonah lifted his head, and his gaze landed on the scorched earth and pile of rubble from the fire. "Not too much. I'm figuring out some stuff." He exhaled slowly before diving in. He'd discuss the fire after he got something more important off his chest. "What did you do when you got back from Iraq to get your head on straight? I need to figure out how to deal with my PTSD. I can't go on living with all this turmoil simmering under the surface. I hoped being back on familiar territory would help, but it's not fixing anything. I need to do more."

"Okay." Dylan stretched the word, and then whistled low under his breath. "I get it, I really do. I don't mean to get all sentimental here, but I'm proud of you. I took close to a year to realize I couldn't fix my problems on my own, and I didn't see half of what you did."

He rubbed a hand through the scruff on his chin. "What did you do? What got you back to normal?"

"I don't know if anyone's ever called me normal." Dylan chuckled. "Honestly, the thing that helped the most was talking to a therapist. The guy I talked to specialized in ex-military dealing with different levels of PTSD."

"You never told me you talked to someone." Jonah twisted toward Dylan and stared at his friend. The idea of Dylan sitting in an office with a stranger and baring his soul was as hard to imagine as a grizzly bear drinking tea with the queen.

Dylan rubbed the back of his neck. "I never told

anyone except my parents. I didn't want everyone in town talking about my business."

"Does he practice at the Veterans Hospital? Do you think I could get an appointment?" He fought to keep the desperation from his voice.

"His practice is around here. The VA was too far of a commute to make twice a week. His name is Dr. St. John. He's a good guy and usually makes military guys a priority."

A sigh of relief escaped from his constricted throat. "Getting his contact information would be great."

"Why the sudden need to see someone? The Jonah I know would fight any help tooth and nail."

He shrugged. "The longer I go without asking for help, the more helpless I feel. If I want to look forward to whatever the future holds, I need to deal with the past."

"I agree. I'll text you his number." Dylan grabbed his phone and stared at his screen for a few seconds.

Jonah's phone buzzed in his pocket. "Thanks, D. I owe you one." Just the thought of the number being in his phone brought him peace. A sense of finally grabbing the bull by the horns and facing his problems head on puffed his chest.

"Owe me for what? You're the one who'll do all the work."

"True. How about I owe you for keeping your mouth shut?"

Dylan clapped a hand on Jonah's shoulder. "You've got it. Your business stays between us."

The front door creaked, and soft-soled shoes shuffled across the ancient wood and stopped directly behind him.

"How are you today, Jonah?"

Meg's voice held a mixture of concern and annoyance. Jonah kept his gaze fixed in front of him. "Not great. Did you talk to Blake?"

Dylan's body tensed.

Jonah twisted to glance up at Meg. Red-rimmed eyes and a pale face stared down at him. Meg looked worse than he felt.

"After I called Dylan last night, I searched for him, but he took off. Dylan said he'd go with me to the police station this morning." Meg crossed her arms over her chest and cocked her hip to the side. "Have you talked to Jillian?"

He gritted his teeth and shook his head. "I can't believe you're taking Jillian's side on this, Meg."

"Don't be an idiot. I'm always on your side, no matter what. But you were harsh as hell last night. I'm sure finding out she was pregnant when she knew you wouldn't be around wasn't easy."

"I didn't abandon her," he snapped. He jumped up and threw his hands in the air.

Nora hopped beside him and whined, flitting her gaze from him to Meg and back again.

Frustration threatened to crack the thin leash he held around his emotions. "I left for boot camp. I'd have come back for both her and the baby when I could. She never gave me a chance."

"From what I know, she didn't have much of a chance either," Meg said quietly. "Did you ask her how she lost the baby?"

Pain pierced his heart, and he swallowed hard. "I was in shock, and I didn't want to hear her excuses. What happened doesn't matter anymore."

"What she went through might not change anything, but put yourself in her shoes. She lost something, too, and she's carried that loss for a long time." Meg slumped forward her shoulders and dropped her gaze to the ground.

Bitterness bit the back of his throat. "I would have carried around the loss for just as long if I'd known. But I didn't."

"You're right," Dylan said. "And who knows if it'd be better or worse. You've dealt with enough loss. But what's done is done and holding on to this anger isn't good for anyone."

"How am I supposed to let go of the anger when the woman I planned on spending the rest of my life with lied? Maybe she was a scared kid when this happened, but she isn't any longer. She's a grown woman, and she should have found a way to tell me."

Meg patted Nora's head.

Dylan ran his fingers through his beard.

Neither had an answer. The wind whipped around the yard and rustled the remaining leaves in the trees.

"Everything will get better. It always does." Dylan got to his feet. "I'm getting my keys, and we'll head to the police station, Meg."

Jonah glanced at Meg and hitched up his lip in a sad, half-smile. "I don't know if I believe my life will get better. This situation with Jillian feels different."

Meg bit into her bottom lip and twirled the end of her braid between her fingers. "Maybe you need to ask yourself why."

He leaned against the porch rail, and the old wood creaked. His mind spun, and he wished for one damn minute all of the noise inside his brain would stop.

"What do you mean?"

"Dylan's right. You've had a lot of loss in your life, and you couldn't do anything about it. But you have a say this time. Jillian isn't being ripped away." Meg firmed her lips and lifted her chin. "You chose to walk away."

His jaw dropped. "I can't be with Jillian because of her actions. Damn, Meg, when did you become such a fan of Jillian's?"

"She shouldn't be persecuted for a tragic event that happened twelve years ago. You've both lost enough." She rested a hand on his arm. "Do you really need to lose each other, too?"

His heart thundered in his chest, and he pinched the bridge of his nose. Too many emotions whirled around in his mind. He couldn't sort them all out. "I don't want to talk about Jillian anymore."

Meg snorted. "What's new? You never want to talk about anything. Don't you think your attitude might be part of your problem?"

He dropped his hands to his sides. He didn't want to talk to anyone about his experience in Iraq, and his PTSD plagued him. He didn't want to talk to Jillian about their baggage from the past, and that'd bitten him in the butt. He reached into his pocket and grabbed his phone. He pulled up the text Dylan sent earlier and stared. "You're right."

"Wait, what?" Meg reared back her head and tented her brows. "I must not have heard you right. Can you say that again?"

He kicked out a foot and pressed lightly on the tip of her black sneaker. "Shut up." He took a deep breath. "If you tell anyone what I'm about to tell you, I'll kill you, but I talked to Dylan when I got here about finding a therapist."

Meg arched an eyebrow and cleared her throat. "Come again?"

"Dylan talked to a therapist when he left the Marines, and this guy specializes in PTSD. I'm making an appointment. Talking to him might not fix everything, but it won't hurt."

"That's great, Jonah." She lifted the side of her mouth. "Will you talk about Jillian?"

Dread pooled in his stomach. He lifted his shoulders. "Seeing a therapist isn't about her. I need help to move on. Finally finding peace might mean moving on from Jillian as well."

Meg nodded. "If that's really what you want."

He rubbed a hand over his face. "I don't know what the hell I want. All I know is, I need to help myself deal with my emotions before I can think about a future with anyone."

Meg tucked her lips up at the corners, and then she disappeared inside the house.

He stared at the open door. The lie he told his baby sister tasted bitter on his tongue. He knew exactly what he wanted—Jillian. The question was, could he ever get over her lie of omission? The possibility was hard to imagine.

He hovered a finger over the number scrawled across his phone. He pressed down on the screen and lifted the device to his ear. A recorded message played, followed by a loud beep.

"Hi, my name is Jonah Sheffield, and I retired from the United States Marine Corps in August. I'm having a difficult time coping with my Post Traumatic Stress

Disorder. I'd like to come in and talk to Dr. St. John as soon as possible. I need his help."

He gave his contact information, and then put his phone back in his pocket. The knot in his stomach loosened. He'd taken the first step toward recovery. A long road stretched ahead with no guarantee of what was at the end.

Chapter Twenty-Four

"Oh my goodness, Jillian. The store is absolutely perfect! Did you think the renovation would turn out this spectacular?" Catie flitted around the newly completed store and ran the tips of her fingers along the spines of the books lining the shelves.

Jillian spun a wide circle. Pride swelled in her chest. Jonah was right. Gus finished before the worst week of her life ended. Two days were needed to paint, one day for the baseboards and trim to go up, and one day to lay down the hickory hardwood floors. She'd changed her mind about the carpet. The wood floors matched Kiddy Korner and added to the cozy, welcoming atmosphere she'd strived for. Now, exactly ten days after the bottom fell out of her world, her new store was ready.

Books Above would open tomorrow, but even though every single thing Jillian bought was exactly where she wanted it, something was missing. She tapped an index finger against her chin and moved down the rows of shelves. She'd categorized the books correctly, and no dust lingered on their spines. She made her way to the fireplace and her heels *click-click-clacked* against the hardwood. Resting her hands on the back of the brown leather sofa, she smoothed the cashmere blanket under her palms and sighed.

"What's wrong?" Catie came up beside her. "You

should be excited about what you've accomplished. Everyone will love this as much as I do. I have no doubt the store will be a success."

Jillian tried to muster a smile for her friend, but her lips curved into what probably looked like a grimace instead. She was proud, but Jonah not sharing in this moment tampered her excitement. Her gaze landed on the spot on the floor where she and Jonah laid not long ago. She inhaled a shaky breath. She would not cry anymore.

Straightening her spine and strengthening her resolve, Jillian tore her gaze from the floor and locked her gaze on Catie. Enthusiasm all but bubbled from her best friend. Her full lips hadn't stopped smiling since they'd come upstairs, and her wide hazel eyes sparkled with excitement. Jillian grabbed Catie's hand and squeezed, hoping some of Catie's eagerness rubbed off. "Nothing's wrong. Everything looks perfect. I can't believe the store's finally done." She pressed a hand to her stomach and curved her lips into a full smile. "I'm anxious about opening tomorrow. I hope everything goes well."

"She's been like this all week," Sam said.

She whirled to find him standing in front of Antonio at the top of the stairs. Sam could always detect her sour mood, which made her disguise her stress even more. Her attempt to hide her feelings never worked.

"I've had a lot on my mind." She nodded toward Antonio, and then skirted around the couch to sit. "What are you two doing here?"

"Dad wanted to see the store." Sam crossed the room and sat on her lap.

She wrapped her arms around him and hugged him close, taking in the familiar scent of his minty shampoo. He hated when she was upset and gave her extra snuggles. The reason for his actions sucked, but she would take the extra attention without complaint. Soon, she'd have to steal them from an unpredictable teenager.

"Is it all right we came?" Antonio stayed by the stairs, and darted his gaze between her and Catie.

"Of course," Jillian answered.

"Have they found Blake yet?" Catie asked.

Earlier, Jillian filled her in on the all the drama, and Catie's fury had yet to die down over what Blake and Antonio did.

Antonio shook his head. "I don't think so." He shifted his weight, and his cheeks sank in at the sides.

"I can't believe he took off. They have to find him soon. Poor Meg." Jillian hadn't talked to Meg, but if Blake had disappeared, then her scumbag fiancé fled without telling Meg where.

Catie snorted. "She dodged a bullet. She can do so much better."

"Maybe Sam and I should go."

Antonio spoke slowly, as if he needed to keep his tone measured so he wouldn't make anyone mad. His behavior almost made her laugh. Catie was a pit bull about protecting her friends, and Antonio was well aware of this. He'd been on the receiving end of her sharp-as-knives tongue before.

Sam wiggled against her and tucked his head under her chin. "I don't want to leave yet."

"Please, stay," Jillian said. "Look around. The place has changed a lot since you've seen it."

"The store looks great, Jillian, but I don't think anyone ever doubted it would. The place will be a madhouse tomorrow when you open. Are you excited?" Antonio strolled around the perimeter of the store. He shoved his hands in his pockets.

"Yeah. I hope the opening goes well."

Antonio halted his movements and glanced at her. He narrowed his eyes and pinched his eyebrows together. "You don't sound convinced."

"Mom's sad," Sam said. "Nothing will cheer her up. I've tried."

Antonio buried his hands so far into his pockets Jillian was afraid he'd burst through the seams.

He hunched forward his shoulders and rocked back on his heels. "Have you talked to Jonah?"

The sound of his name was like a dagger in her heart. She shook her head and bit hard into her bottom lip to keep away the stupid tears.

"Do you really think you should talk about Jonah?"

Catie spoke with the brutal force of a tidal wave. She placed a hard emphasis on every other word to make no mistake on how she thought Antonio should answer her question. Jillian waved her down. "He's fine. No, I haven't."

Antonio fixed his gaze to the floor, and he twisted his lips to the side. "Have you tried?"

Jillian squeezed her arms tighter around Sam. Even though she'd agreed with Annie about her and Jonah both needing closure, she couldn't bring herself to call. The conversation wouldn't be easy, and she wasn't ready to hammer down the final nail in their relationship. "He doesn't want to talk to me."

Sam twisted to face her with wide eyes. "You

always tell me if I have a problem, I need to face it head on. Maybe that's what you need to do with Jonah."

Catie chuckled. "The kid's got a point. Jonah doesn't have to talk if he doesn't want to, but you have a right to get things off your chest."

They were both right. She had put off the inevitable long enough. A surge of determination rushed through her, and she set Sam on his feet before she stood. She had to act now before she again lost her nerve. "I need to talk to Jonah, and I need to do it now. Sam, you have a good night at your dad's, and I'll see you tomorrow. Catie, I'll call you later." She bent down, kissed Sam on the forehead, and rushed down the stairs before she could talk herself out of leaving. The need to see Jonah nearly overwhelmed her, but she stomped down the lingering doubts and fears. She would tell Jonah everything, even if his chilly reception destroyed her.

****

A light dusting of snow covered the ground, and a trail of Jillian's footprints wrapped around her car. Snow arrived early this year to Smithview, but that didn't mean it would stay. This snow in early October could quickly turn into a hot, humid day with a snap of her fingers. Ohio weather often spanned all four seasons in just as many days. Maybe meeting Jonah outside wasn't her best idea. Her light jacket wouldn't help much against the sudden winter-like temperatures.

But she couldn't back down. She'd texted Jonah and asked him to meet her at the dam—the same spot that dominated so many of her memories. His lack of response worried her, but she'd wait as long as she could. She opened the trunk of her car and grabbed two blankets. They'd keep away the cold while she waited. She clutched her keys in one hand as she closed the trunk with the other. As the cold metal of the keys branded the palm of her hand, she curved her lips into a small smile. At least she wouldn't lock herself out of her car this time.

She followed the trail down to the dam. She clutched the blankets and the picture frame she'd grabbed from home to her chest. Her boots crunched along the path. Thank God, she had changed out of her heels before she'd left. The wind whipped across her face, and she hurried along until she found a bench in a small clearing in front of the dam. She draped one of the blankets over the bench, sat, and huddled under the second one.

The water cascaded over the opening, and then gurgled along down the river. It thundered in her ears, and she concentrated on the falling snowflakes hitting the sprays of water and melting into one. The chaos of the falling water shifting into the peaceful stream calmed her nerves. That's why she'd asked Jonah to meet her here—to join her at their spot. She needed a place she could collect her thoughts. And maybe…just maybe…memories of the time they'd spent here together would soften his heart enough to listen.

Her lips chattered, and the impending numbness made her ears tingle. She should have grabbed a hat. The bright, blue sky and glaring sunlight tricked her. She stared at the frame resting in her lap. The frame was small, but it was her peace offering. She wasn't naïve enough to think what it held would change where they stood, but hopefully, the gift would be enough to give them both closure. Tears splattered down on the glass, and she heaved a heavy sigh. Her heart cracked in two.

Straightening her spine, she willed the tears to stop falling. She couldn't fall apart again. She had Sam, and that was enough. Being a mom had to be enough, because she'd never love another man the way she loved Jonah. Trying to love someone else had been a mistake. She wouldn't try again.

A twig snapped in the woods behind her, and she whipped around her head. The frame fell to the ground as her heart dropped to her feet. She sucked in a loud breath, and a bead of sweat formed at her brow. She wasn't ready yet. She needed more time to sort out her thoughts—needed more time to figure out the right words to say.

His deep, blue eyes met hers and widened. He stopped, and time stood still. Finally, he started toward her again. The material of his jacket bunched around the hands in his pockets, and his gaze stayed glued to his feet.

He'd come. The roar of the dam faded into the background, and her pulse thundered wildly through her ears. She couldn't take her gaze off him.

He rounded the bench and stood in front of her, blocking the sun and casting a long shadow.

She tilted her head to see his face. Her heart screamed in her chest.

He arched his brows. "What happened? Lock yourself out of your car again?"

Butterflies dive-bombed against her stomach lining, and she sucked in a deep breath. She would have this conversation, even if it killed her.

Chapter Twenty-Five

Despite the cold, Jonah fought his nerves, his palms growing moist in his pockets. He locked his gaze with Jillian's, and his heart constricted in his chest. He'd just left his first therapy session, and his stomach coiled into knots when Jillian's text scrawled across his phone. She hadn't left his mind once since he'd seen her last. The time had come to talk.

He shifted and the sun streamed down, illuminating the freckles scattered on her face. A gust of wind whipped her hair across her cheek, and he shot out his hand and tucked the golden strands behind her ear. The satiny skin on her cheek tickled his fingers. Jolts of electricity shot up his arm. He quickly dropped his hand to his side.

She lowered her gaze, and then bent over to pick up something off the ground. She laid it in her lap and wiped the snow off with her blanket. "I kept my keys with me this time."

He glanced upward and watched for a moment as the white flakes landed on the brightly colored leaves still clinging to the trees. He'd missed this crazy weather. "Do you always ask people to meet you in the snow when you have something to talk about?"

"Only when I can't think of a better place to go." She lifted her gaze to meet his.

His mouth went dry, and his heart pounded. "Can I

237

sit?"

Nodding, she scooted over on the bench and lifted the far end of the blanket.

He sat and nestled his thigh close before he tucked the blanket over his lap.

She faced him. "I have a few things I need to talk about."

Pain shone clearly through her red-rimmed eyes. "Okay." He braced himself, and the muscles in his shoulders clenched together.

She took a deep breath and lifted her fingers to brush away the tears that clung to her cheeks. "You were right. I should have tried harder to tell you about the baby—back then and now. I found out I was pregnant the day you left for boot camp. That's way I never came to say goodbye. I was in shock, and by the time I pulled myself together and reached your house, you were already gone. I must have written you a hundred letters, but telling you I was pregnant in a letter didn't feel right. I needed to tell you in person. Looking back, I know you had no control over where you could be or when. But I was young and scared and didn't think about how long it might be before I could see you."

"But keeping it from me was okay?" His words lacked the anger they had before. Anger was useless. Holding onto it only postponed the bitter pain it kept at bay.

A small gasp parted her lips. "Nothing feels right without you, Jonah. I planned to tell you about the pregnancy when you came home, but you never did. I wrote you and let you know I had something to tell you, but you never responded. I guessed you were done with me."

Her words were small, as if lodged in the throat, and punched him in the gut. "I was confused and angry and heartbroken. Your letter didn't come for six weeks. Boot camp was hard enough, but throw in the torture of wondering what happened the day I left..." He shrugged. "I never read your letter. I was too angry. When nothing else ever came, I gave up on us."

Jillian scrunched together her face and dropped her gaze to her lap. "I figured you'd moved on or found someone else while you were gone. I was determined to go on without you and raise our child on my own. Once I lost her..." Her voice cracked, and she wrapped her arms around her stomach. She closed her eyes, and her breath spiraled in the air in soft wisps. "The pain was so bad. I'd never met or got to hold her, but I loved her so much. My heart shattered into a million pieces, and it's never been whole since. I will always have a hole there, and I will never forget the small life you and I created. But if I could spare you the pain..."

The familiar scents of vanilla and lavender filled his lungs and steadied his nerves, even as his chest tightened. He wrapped an arm around her shoulders and pressed her tight against him. He nuzzled his face against her hair and breathed her in. "It was a girl? What happened?" He could barely speak louder than a whisper, and tears clogged his throat.

Tears streamed freely down her face. "I still hadn't told anyone about her. I wasn't showing when I went in for my twenty-week appointment. My young age and good genes were a blessing in that regard." She sniffed, and a soft laugh gurgled low in her throat. "I went in to find out the gender, and they couldn't find a heartbeat.

One second she was there…and then she was gone. All the hopes and dreams I'd had for her, and for us, were dashed as soon as I saw the look on the doctor's face." Jillian took a deep breath before she continued. "Because I was so far along, I needed to have a procedure done to remove the fetus. I hadn't even told anyone I was pregnant, so I didn't have anyone to take me."

"You went by yourself?" Jonah interrupted. Guilt churned in his gut. She'd been through hell, and she'd had no one to lean on. "I would have found a way to be there. You should have reached out and given me a chance."

Jillian smiled through her tears. "I imagined you with me the entire time. If you couldn't be there, I didn't want anyone. I didn't want anyone else to experience our child if you'd never get to know her. So I went by myself, and when they told me she was a girl, I wept for the life she would never have. She was ours, if only for a brief moment in time." She sniffed and wiped the corner of her eyes with the tips of her fingers. "I will remember her forever."

My brave Jillian. He put his hands on her face and pressed his lips to hers. He tasted the salty tears on her lips. His body hummed with excitement, and he dropped his hands to her arms and lifted his mouth. His eyes misted, and he gathered her into his arms.

She lifted her head from his shoulder. "Oh geez, you're a mess. I'm sorry." She wiped her face with a hand.

He lifted the corner of his mouth. "I'll manage." He tugged down his lips in a slight frown, and he linked his fingers in hers. Her fingers were freezing, but the feel of her skin warmed his heart. "Did you name her?" A small light brightened Jillian's green eyes.

"I called her Lily James. You and I joked once about what we would name our kids. Do you remember? We both liked Lily for a girl, and I thought having James after your dad would be nice."

His chest pinched. The tears he'd held in finally broke free.

Jillian gathered him into her embrace, and together, they mourned the loss of their tiny daughter.

A sharp edge dug into his side, and he pulled away. He wiped his face and sniffed, pulling himself together. "Whatever you're holding just punctured my ribs."

Jillian grabbed a tissue from her pocket and dabbed her nose. "I completely forgot. I have something for you." She extended a silver frame.

His heart dropped. He brushed his fingers against the glass holding the picture in place and sucked in a large breath through his nose. "Is this her?"

"That's the first sonogram picture they gave me. I want you to have it so you'll always keep a piece of her with you."

"Thank you." He couldn't tear away his gaze from the picture. He couldn't tell her head from her legs, but it didn't matter. This grainy blob was his daughter. He lifted his head and stared at Jillian. Her eyes were wide and her lips trembled. She wasn't a woman who lied and kept secrets to hurt him. She kept their baby a secret because she loved him, and then mourned the loss of her alone to protect him. He might never understand her actions, but he didn't doubt they came from a place of love.

Clearing her throat, she dropped her gaze and

picked a stray piece of lint from the blanket. "I'm glad you like it. I should probably head home now. Sam will be there soon. Thank you for hearing me out. It's long past time I told you what happened." She stood, keeping her gaze focused downward.

He closed his hand around hers, palm to palm, and pulled her in front of him. He parted his legs, placing one knee on either side of her. The blanket bunched on his lap, and he threw it to the ground. His other hand closed around her hip. "Jilly," he whispered.

She tucked her bottom lip beneath her teeth. "Please, Jonah, don't make goodbye harder than it has to be. Walking away will take all my strength."

No way could he let her walk away. He tightened his hand on her hip before pulling her to him. Her breasts pressed against his chest, and he leaned his forehead to hers. His heart raced, and he placed their joined hands on top of it. The fanatical rhythm of his heart beat beneath them. "I don't want you to walk away." He spoke low, keeping his voice tender.

Her eyes flew open. "But you said—"

"I know what I said." He shook his head. "I was hurt and angry as hell. I never stopped to think about what you went through or the reasons behind your decisions. I don't agree with all of your choices, but I know you never meant to hurt me."

"I never wanted to hurt you."

He cupped her cheek and brushed the pad of his thumb across it to wipe it dry. "I'm sorry I hurt you, too." Apprehension sat heavy in his gut. Maybe he'd hurt her too bad and ruined any chance of a future, but he had to give it one more shot. "Do you think we can try again? This time with a clean slate and all our cards on the table?"

A giggle bubbled out of her throat, and she threw her arms around his neck. "Yes, yes, absolutely yes."

Huffing out a breath, he wrapped his arms around her and clasped his hands together at the small of her back. He finally had her back, and this time he would never let her go. "I love you so damn much, Jillian."

"I love you, too. If it's possible, I love you more than I did twelve years ago."

Her muffled breath was hot against his neck and warmed him down to his toes. "Definitely possible. Didn't you know? Everything's sweeter the second time around."

Epilogue

The months leading to Christmas were the happiest Jonah could remember. Jillian's new store exceeded her expectations, he got his contractor's license, and Sam was more receptive to him being a permanent part of his life.

On the first day of winter break, he took Sam out for a guys' day. He'd promised Sam he could pick anywhere he wanted to go for lunch. He also promised a game of laser tag once they finished eating.

After they took their seats at their table in the Mexican restaurant Sam chose, he glanced at Sam and asked him the question weighing on his mind. "How are you feeling about everything with me and your mom?"

"I feel fine." Sam studied the menu.

"I need you to focus, buddy. What I have to say is important."

Sam set down his menu and folded his hands.

"Are you happy I'm in your mom's life and in your life?"

Sam wrinkled his nose. "I think so. I like spending time with you, and I can see how happy my mom is when you're around." He paused. "She gets a little sad when you leave."

"Do you like it when I leave?" His stomach was a quivering mess as he waited for Sam's answer. They'd made a lot of progress, and hearing Sam didn't want him around would kill him.

Sam gave a small shrug. "Not really. But when you're at our house, you don't leave until after I'm already asleep."

He relaxed into his seat. Leaving Sam after he was already in bed was very different from tearing himself away from Jillian at night. "How would you feel about me being at your house all the time?"

Sam pursed his lips and narrowed his eyes. "Like you'd move in?"

Jonah nodded and steepled his hands on the table. Blood pounded in his ears. His question was the main reason he wanted to have time alone with Sam today. If Sam didn't want him to move in, he was screwed. "Yes."

Sam lifted a shoulder. "I guess that'd be okay."

"I wouldn't move in for a while still. I would have to ask your mom first."

Sam tilted his head to the side. "You haven't asked my mom yet? How do you know she'd be okay with it?"

He couldn't hold back any longer. A bark of laughter escaped from his throat. "I wanted to make sure you were okay with my asking before I asked her. I won't bring it up to your mom if you don't want me there. But I need to ask you something else."

"What?"

He took a deep breath. "I really want to live with you and your mom, but I want to marry your mom first. Do I have your permission to ask her to marry me?"

Sam's eyes shot wide open. "You're asking for my permission?"

"Of course I am. You're the most important person

in her life, and I can't ask her to marry me if I don't have your blessing first."

Sam's chest puffed up. "Asking would be all right. I think she would like getting married."

Relief loosened the tension in his chest. "I think so, too. Now, I have one more question."

"Another one?" Sam leaned his head back against the seat, and his shoulders drooped.

Jonah chuckled and widened his eyes. "Yep, one more. Will you help me pick out the ring?"

"Sure." Sam smiled. "I know what Mom likes."

When the food arrived, Jonah sat back for a minute and watched the boy he'd grown to love dive into his meal. His heart constricted at the thought of his family growing by not just one person, but by two. He couldn't believe his luck. From where he sat, his future looked pretty damn good.

****

Tattered wrapping paper littered the space on the ground between toys, new clothes, and the heaps of other opened presents. For once, Jillian didn't care about the mess. She sat on the floor in her favorite, red-and-black plaid pajamas and sipped her coffee. The white lights sparkled against the green evergreen needles, and happiness warmed her body more efficiently than the warm, sweet liquid from her mug.

Jonah strolled into the living room and leaned forward to kiss her forehead. "Having a Merry Christmas?"

She smiled and moved against him with her gaze locked on Sam building an elaborate world of blocks by the tree. "I've had a perfect Christmas with you and Sam, but I still feel bad for not exchanging gifts. I wish

I hadn't agreed to no presents between us this year."

"Would you be mad if I changed my mind about getting you something?"

Excitement and guilt clashed in her gut, and she playfully slapped Jonah's arm. "Why didn't you tell me you changed your mind? I hate not having a present to give you."

Standing, Jonah smiled and cleared his throat.

Sam jumped to his feet and hurried to Jonah's side.

Jillian furrowed her brow and bounced her gaze from the man she loved to her darling son. Mischief oozed from Sam's wide grin. What were they up to?

Jonah plunged his hand in his pocket and pulled out a ring box.

Jillian's breath caught in her throat, and she covered her mouth with shaking hands. "What did you do?"

"Not just Jonah, Mom." Sam bounced on his toes. "I helped with everything. I even picked out the—"

Jonah poked him with his elbow. "Wait a second. Let me say a few things before you spill all of my secrets."

Sam laughed. "Sorry."

To hide a laugh, Jillian bit into her bottom lip. Sam keeping anything a surprise was a shock, especially something this big. Her thoughts spun at a rapid speed, nearly as fast as her frantically beating heart.

Jonah lowered himself to one knee and grabbed Jillian's hand. "Honey, I never imagined I would ever be this happy again. Not just with you, but with Sam. I've loved you since I was a kid, and finding my way back to you after all these years is nothing short of a miracle. You've brought the light back to my life, and I never want to live without you—or Sam—again. Will you grant my Christmas wish and agree to be my wife?"

Jillian flung herself into Jonah's arms. She'd waited her entire life for this moment. Tears burned in her eyes, and joy bubbled inside her chest. She hadn't thought life could be any better, but she was wrong. She would be Mrs. Jonah Sheffield. "Absolutely! I would love nothing more than to marry you."

Jonah circled his arms around her and held her close. He pressed his lips to her ear. "Do you want to see the ring?"

She giggled and wiggled from his grasp. She fixed her gaze on the small black box.

He lifted the lid and pinched his fingers around the ring. Then he slid the band on her finger.

Pulse racing, Jillian stared down at a gold band with a large, round diamond in the middle.

"Do you like the ring?" Sam dropped to his knees and stared at her hand. "I told Jonah you'd want something simple."

Love filled her chest, and the tears hovering over lashes spilled over. "You helped Jonah with the ring, huh?"

Sam lifted his chest. "He asked my permission to marry you, and then we went ring shopping."

A lump clogged her throat. Jillian locked her gaze on Jonah's. This man knew her whole heart. How had she gotten so lucky to not only rekindle the love of her life but have him love her son as well?

Jonah tousled Sam's hair. "I couldn't ask you to marry me without this guy's permission. He's the man of the house, after all."

Jillian grinned and wrapped one arm around each of her favorite people, pulling them close. "I love you both so much. Our life together will be filled with happiness, fun, and a little bit of craziness."

Jonah kissed her lips then grinned. "I wouldn't have it any other way."

A word about the author...

Danielle M. Haas resides in Ohio with her husband and two children. She earned a BA in Political Science many moons ago from Bowling Green State University, but thought staying home with her two children and writing romance novels would be more fun than pursuing a career in politics.

She is a member of Romance Writers of America, as well as her local North East Ohio chapter. She spends her days chasing her kids around, loving up her dog, and trying to find a spare minute to write about her favorite thing: love.

Danielle can be found blogging about her adventures in writing at www.daniellemhaas.com, via her Facebook page under Author Danielle Haas, or you can follow her twitter handle, @authordhaas.

http://www.daniellemhaas.com

CPSIA information can be obtained
at www.ICGtesting.com
Printed in the USA
BVHW050009300721
612898BV00008B/590

9 781509 228935